# About the author

Elen Caldecott graduated with an MA in Writing for Young People from Bath Spa University. Before becoming a writer, she was an archaeologist, a nurse, a theatre usher and a museum security guard. It was while working at the museum that Elen realised there is a way to steal anything if you think about it hard enough. Elen either had to become a master thief, or create some characters to do it for her – and so her debut novel, *How Kirsty Jenkins Stole the Elephant*, was born. It was shortlisted for the Waterstones Children's Prize and was followed by *The Mystery of Wickworth Manor*, *The Great Ice-Cream Heist* and most recently *The Marsh Road Mysteries*. Elen lives in Bristol with her husband, Simon, and their dog.

**www.elencaldecott.com**

Che...               ...Children's Author page
on Facebook

# Also by Elen Caldecott

# DOGS *and* DOCTORS

*The*

## MARSH ROAD
MYSTERIES

# DOGS
*and*

# DOCTORS

## ELEN CALDECOTT

**BLOOMSBURY**
LONDON  OXFORD  NEW YORK  NEW DELHI  SYDNEY

Bloomsbury Publishing, London, Oxford, New York, New Delhi and Sydney

First published in Great Britain in May 2017 by Bloomsbury Publishing Plc
50 Bedford Square, London WC1B 3DP

www.bloomsbury.com
www.elencaldecott.com

A CIP catalogue record for this book is available from the British Library

ISBN 978 1 4088 7606 0

Typeset by RefineCatch Limited, Bungay, Suffolk
Printed and bound in Great Britain by CPI Group (UK) Ltd, Croydon CR0 4YY

1 3 5 7 9 10 8 6 4 2

*To Otis, with love*

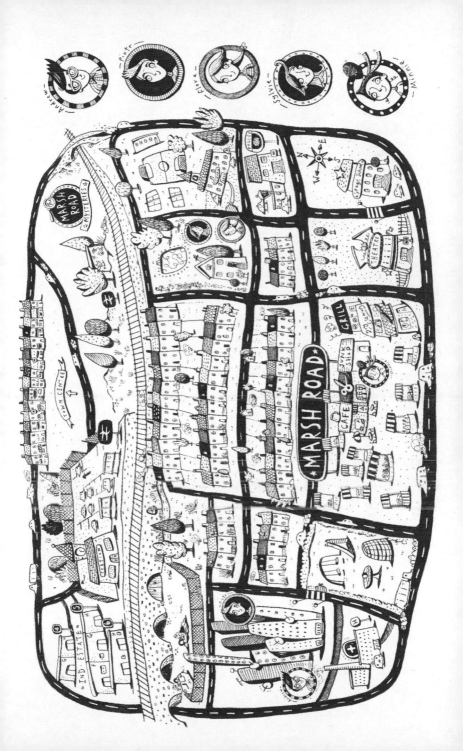

# Chapter One

Sylvie Hampshire had blood on her hands. Cherry-red pinpricks of blood. She scowled, at the world in general, and at Dr Malcolm in particular.

'I am not a baked potato,' she said, 'you don't have to stab me full of holes.'

'Sorry,' Dr Malcolm said.

Sylvie thought *contempt*. She thought *disgust*. At acting classes the teacher said that if you thought an emotion, it would appear on your face. Sylvie thought *irritation* very hard indeed.

'Sylvie,' Mum warned, 'Dr Malcolm is only trying to help.'

He was not. He was trying to steal her blood and then order her to eat, or not eat, or inject insulin. He was like a vampire playing Simon Says. And she was sick of it.

She thought *sick of it*.

Mum sighed. 'You see, Dr Malcolm, Sylvie is under the impression that she can manage her own treatment. She wants to do her own blood tests every day and decide for herself what to do about the results. With no help at all from anyone else.' Mum sounded as worried as she had when Sylvie had first suggested it, weeks ago.

'I see.' Dr Malcolm turned to look at his computer, avoiding both their stares. He tugged at his collar. It was as though his calming, soothing, tastefully decorated office was suddenly cramped, small, poky. As though the abstract painting on the wall – blue bleeding into red, via purple – was too much like a close-up of veins and arteries. Mum's glare could have that effect on people, though not on Sylvie, whose stare was just as stern.

Sylvie sucked the drops of blood from her fingertip. 'It's high time I did it myself,' she told him. 'Mum chooses my meals and packs my lunch. She checks up to see if I've done blood tests, even if I already have. She nags me to rotate the injection site – like I was five years old and doing it for the first time! Dr Malcolm, I'm not a baby any more.'

Dr Malcolm tapped his keyboard. He was still wearing his plastic gloves. He never took them off. They squeaked annoyingly against the plastic keys. It set her teeth on edge.

He finally looked up. 'Ms Hampshire, I've been taking a look at Sylvie's records. We've been managing her diabetes well for the last year. Do you think Sylvie might be responsible enough to take over her day-to-day management?'

'Responsible?' Mum sounded confused. 'She's never managed to pick up her own dirty clothes from the bedroom floor and put them in the laundry basket.'

'This is different!' Sylvie said. 'I *want* to do this!'

'No one wants to do laundry,' Mum said softly.

Dr Malcolm steepled his fingertips together and was doing his best to look as though he was in charge, but a pink flush was spreading across his face like blancmange being tipped on to a tablecloth. He was probably wondering how one of the leading specialists in childhood type 1 diabetes, a world-renowned endocrinologist, had become involved in a row about laundry.

'I have a suggestion,' he said.

'We're listening,' Mum said cautiously.

'It's something we've tried very successfully with other patients Sylvie's age,' he said. 'I propose a trial. Let's put Sylvie in charge of her own management. She'll do her own finger-prick tests at least three times a day, and her own insulin injections twice a day. She will also manage her own mealtimes with no nagging from anyone.'

'Dr Malcolm!' Mum gasped.

'Yes!' Sylvie punched the air.

'Wait, I haven't finished.' Dr Malcolm held up his hand. 'Sylvie does all this by herself, but she stays on hospital grounds for forty-eight hours while she does it. We'll take her on to the children's ward. It's half-term, isn't it? So she won't miss any school.'

Mum looked at Sylvie.

Sylvie looked at Mum.

It was easy to know what Mum was thinking, because the look of shock in her blue eyes matched perfectly how Sylvie was feeling herself.

'It might be all right,' Mum said cautiously. 'Sylvie might be able to show she's growing up ...'

What? In hospital, where staff watched you all the time? Where they asked you stupid questions about how you felt? As if you could feel anything other than totally miserable sharing a room with five other kids and a whole load of toys with pieces missing – one-armed dolls and jigsaws that only made half a picture. No. Hospital was the worst place in the world, bar none.

Her eyes narrowed. Why was Dr Malcolm being so mean? 'I don't need to be on the ward. You said I've been managing well. You just said.'

Dr Malcolm checked his screen. 'There's an empty bed right now. We can begin the trial whenever you like.'

Trial?

Sylvie crossed her arms, gripping her elbows fiercely. This was a trial – as though she were being punished for something she hadn't even done. But she was innocent! And she was being sent to the primary-coloured prison of the children's ward. This wasn't fair.

'I don't want to!' she said.

'You don't want to manage your own treatment?' Dr Malcolm asked mildly.

'No! I do,' she replied. He wasn't even listening!

'Then that's settled. I'll book you in now and you can go along there at any point today to settle in. In two days, we'll discuss how it's all gone. How's that?'

Mum gave bird-like nods, sharp and uncertain.

Sylvie didn't nod at all.

Dr Malcolm was the only one who seemed pleased. 'Don't forget, Sylvie. Three tests, two injections and, most importantly, regular meals, every day.'

Sylvie stared at the ugly painting with its blue and red streaks. These were her last moments of freedom.

\* \* \*

Outside Dr Malcolm's office, Sylvie's twin sister, Flora, sat on a huge padded chair and turned the page of her book. She hoped Mum and Sylvie would take a while longer, because the detective in the mystery was just on the point of revealing whodunit, and Flora wanted to check that her guess was right. The twins and their friends Piotr, Andrew and Minnie had become pretty good sleuths since they'd met. They had found stolen jewels, unmasked smugglers and spies and even foiled a curse. Flora bet she was right about the mild-mannered librarian in the book.

But, just as the detective had invited everyone into the drawing room to reveal the identity of the criminal, Dr Malcolm's door opened.

Sylvie stormed out and glowered at her twin. How could Flora just sit there when she was about to be locked up on near-death row? 'I'm not allowed to come home,' Sylvie said. 'I'm being incarcerated against my will.'

'What?' Flora closed her book.

Sylvie explained Dr Malcolm's cruel and unusual plan. Flora didn't react.

'You don't seem bothered. Do you want me to be locked up here?' Sylvie demanded.

'It's only for two days. And if you do what they want, then you get what you want.'

Flora was as bad as they were. Sylvie thought *murderous* and glared at her twin.

Mum followed her out of the room. 'Sylvie will need an overnight bag,' she said. 'I'm going to run home and pick up the things she'll need. There's no need for you both to come. You can go straight to the children's ward and I'll meet you there.'

Sylvie said nothing.

Flora nodded and put her book away in her backpack.

'Right. Right, then. I'll be half an hour.' Mum hitched her handbag higher and walked away from Dr Malcolm's office.

It was all right for Dr Malcolm. His office was on the third floor of the hospital, up in the quiet and the calm. With its cream walls and olive carpets it felt more like the head offices of a cool juice company than a hospital. Down in the children's ward, where he had condemned her to stay, it was all yelling and crying and moaning and nosy nurses and no privacy whatsoever. Sylvie pulled tongues at his pale oak office door. She dropped down into the seat beside Flora.

'What are you doing?' Flora asked. 'Mum said to meet her on the children's ward.'

'She said to meet her in half an hour. I'm not stepping into that hell until I absolutely have to.'

Flora rolled her eyes and took out her book.

After about twenty minutes of glaring, Sylvie leaped up. 'Right. This way,' she snapped at Flora, who shoved her paperback into her backpack again, quietly satisfied that she'd been right about the librarian.

Sylvie didn't bother to check that Flora was following. They both knew where the ward was. They had both been there a hundred times, though it was only ever Sylvie who had to stay. The fact that she knew the way – practically with her eyes closed – made her cross.

She stomped towards the staircase.

Sylvie gripped the polished banister. The white steps had black trim at the edges, so it was like walking down a piano. On good visits to Dr Malcolm, she'd sometimes sing in this stairwell, because the echo was so nice. Today her mouth clamped shut. Then a sudden jolt made her cry out. 'Hey!'

A man had barrelled past her, head down. Tall, in blue overalls. She didn't see his face, just a flash of pale skin from under his cap. His elbow caught her shoulder.

She was pushed against the wall. 'Hey!' she yelled at his back.

Then she noticed drops of blood. On the stairs. Not hers. Some part of her had noticed his hand. One clutching the other as though it was injured.

She didn't care how hurt his hand was. It wasn't OK to push past her without saying sorry. She broke into a trot, following him. Her shoulder felt bruised where she'd banged the wall. She'd practically been dashed to pieces. 'Say sorry!' she yelled.

But the man sped up. Running now, taking the stairs two at a time. His footfall echoed back up. It sounded like twenty men running.

Sylvie broke into a run too. 'Wait!'

Behind her, Flora called out, 'Sylvie, what are you doing?'

But Sylvie had already taken enough knocks today. She wasn't taking another one lying down.

She pelted after the man with Flora on her heels.

With an injured hand, he must be headed to Minor Injuries on the ground floor. Down one flight, turn, down the next, one more. Footsteps further away.

Ground floor.

She rushed away from the stairs. Where was he? She

craned her head to see past the milling people on their way to Minor Injuries. No one running.

'There!' Flora nudged her side.

The man with the bloody hand hurtled across the atrium, cap bowed against the security cameras, past the surprised-looking guard on the door and out of the building.

# Chapter Two

'He's going the wrong way!' Sylvie called out. 'Hey!' But the man didn't look back. In seconds he was dodging the fountain that stood in front of the hospital, on to the road and gone.

How dare he barge past and not even check she was OK!

He would have been a handy person to have shouted at for a while. It might have made her feel better about being stuck in the hospital. She folded her arms angrily and glared at the two women in neat dark suits behind the reception desk. She glowered at the waiting staff in the cafe, warm behind lit displays of soup and golden pasties. Even the people in the gift shop, labelling up newspaper orders for delivery to the wards, were irritating.

'Come on.' Flora wiggled her hand under Sylvie's

clenched elbow. 'Mum told us we should go straight to the ward.'

Sylvie felt Flora tug at her; she resisted. Flora wasn't the boss.

Flora's grip loosened, became more of a pat. 'Are you all right?'

'No!' Sylvie snapped.

There was a small bench she knew of, tucked behind the stairwell. She pulled away from Flora and slumped down on to it, hidden in the shadow of the wall. The bench had been put there to make it more comfortable to look at a particular painting. Sylvie scowled at the security guard in front of it. He ignored her.

The very first time she'd noticed the painting, she'd been stomping across the atrium with Mum. It had been about four years ago. They'd just met Dr Malcolm and Sylvie hated him. He'd told Sylvie that her diabetes couldn't be cured, only managed, and that she and Mum would have to work hard to keep it under control. She already worked hard. She did extra lessons in dance and drama, as well as everything at school. She hadn't wanted more work. Hadn't wanted to be part of this stupid hospital world. She'd just wanted to be normal.

Well, not normal; she wanted to be famous, but normal famous, not sickly famous.

She'd sulked on the bench while Mum made extra appointments and filled out forms at reception.

And then she'd looked up. And seen the painting of the lilies sparkling in a sun-splattered pond.

And, for a moment, she'd forgotten all about Sylvie Hampshire. She'd been lost at the edge of the water, on a sunny day, in a place that was outside time. She was the blues and greens of the water, the white and yellow of the sunlight on the lily pads. Her limbs relaxed. The knots unbound in her shoulders. For that moment, the illness didn't matter.

But the painting didn't work today. She was too crotchety.

Flora sat beside her. 'That painting belongs to Dame Julie Dent, you know? The actress?'

'It looks a bit cold and wet to me,' Sylvie said.

Flora giggled. 'It does a bit.'

'Why is it here if it belongs to an actress?'

'All the art in the hospital is on loan from different people. It's a scheme. Last time we were here I read a leaflet about it.'

That didn't surprise Sylvie – her twin would read the

cereal packet at breakfast if there was nothing else about. They sat in silence for a while. Somehow the bustling sounds of the atrium and the babble of conversation from the cafe began to sound like a distant stream running into a lake. She stared at the soft colours of the canvas.

'Tell me what's the matter,' Flora said.

'I don't want to be here,' Sylvie replied. 'I'm not poorly. Even Dr Malcolm said so. It's not fair.'

'You're just feeling cranky.'

'I'm never cranky! Not unless I have low blood sugar. Or I'm tired. Or bored. Or someone's being annoying. Only then.'

'Yes, only then.' Flora slipped her hand through the crook of Sylvie's elbow and squeezed. A tiny bit of a hug.

Sylvie smiled, even though she didn't want to.

'Shall we go to the ward?' Flora asked.

'If we must.'

They both stood up and headed back towards the stairs.

There was no need to follow the signs; it was as familiar as the streets around their house. But each time they passed a royal-blue sign proudly announcing the way to 'Peter Pan Ward' Sylvie's feet got heavier and heavier, slower and slower.

Flora pressed the buzzer. There was no way Sylvie was going to do it. In moments, the door clicked and they were inside.

The noise! She'd forgotten the noise. Young ones like wind-up dolls, with sticky fingers and missing teeth, chattered and clattered between beds. Older ones called out to each other. Big ones carried a halo of sound, coming tinny from their headphones, some with metal in their eyebrows like oversized staples. Toys were bashed and banged. Machines beeped for the sickest ones.

Sylvie stood stone still.

Flora squished sanitiser on to her hands, then nudged Sylvie to do the same. 'It kills superbugs,' she said simply. It was Flora who went up to the nurses' station to announce their arrival. Sylvie didn't budge.

Flora returned, trailing Nurse Adams. The nurse was short – only a tiny bit taller than Flora – but she was easy to spot. Her eyes were always rimmed with vivid liner in gold or silver, and her hair had a streak of colour that seemed to change nearly every day. Today it was green. Her smile was always the same, though – a show-every-tooth grin.

'Sylvie! Sylvie Hampshire! Back with us again. How are you doing?'

15

Sylvie shrugged. She thought *Ice Queen of Narnia*.

'That well? I was so pleased when I saw your name pop up on the roster. We haven't had a star in here since, well, since the last time you stayed.'

Sylvie felt herself thaw a teensy, tiny bit. It was nice that Nurse Adams recognised her talent.

'I'm only in for observation, you know.'

'You could at least say hello,' Flora said.

'Hello, Nurse Adams. I'm only in for observation, you know.'

'I know. I saw. How exciting. Dr Malcolm says you can come and go as you please, as long as you stay inside the hospital. It will be up to you to remember to come back in good time for meals. Try your best – I know your mum's a lawyer, and we don't want her upset, do we?' Nurse Adams's grin stayed exactly where it was. 'Well, let's get you settled. You've a bed on the ward.'

Nurse Adams swivelled on her white plastic heel and led the way towards a row of beds.

She stopped at an empty one. It was near the window, but every other sick kid on the ward would be walking by to stare out at freedom, so that wasn't great. The white sheets were bound tight to the mattress. A cabinet that was too big to be a side table, but too small to be a wardrobe,

16

squatted next to the bed, somehow managing to look embarrassed. There was a wipe-down plastic chair and a table that went across the bed. If it all got too much, there was a curtain you could pull across to hide from the rest of the world. It had cartoon princesses on it. Some palace.

Sylvie sighed dramatically.

'Caleb,' Nurse Adams said, 'this is your new neighbour, Sylvie Hampshire. She's an old hand. Sylvie, this is Caleb Burroughs.'

Sylvie eyed the boy in the bed next to her with not much curiosity, while Flora rearranged the chair and neatened up the already immaculate cabinet. Nurse Adams yelped as she saw a toddler climb on to a TV stand. She disappeared at a charge.

The boy, Caleb, was pale and very thin. He looked like greaseproof paper wrapped around a coat hanger. He didn't seem to be moving much; only his chest rising up and down gave any sign at all that he was still alive. A small plastic tube was taped to his nostril.

'What's wrong with you?' Sylvie asked.

Flora hushed her.

Caleb didn't say anything.

'You look terrible,' Sylvie tried again.

Caleb turned his head slowly. 'Are you talking to me?'

he whispered. His voice was as dry as paper too.

'Yes, of course,' Sylvie replied. 'What's the matter with you?'

'You are, right now,' Caleb said, and let his eyes close.

Sylvie watched for a second, to see if he did anything else. But there was nothing. 'How rude!' She grabbed hold of the dancing princesses drapes and pulled them hard, shutting off Caleb and the rest of the ward.

She clambered on to the bed, not bothering to take off her shoes.

'Do you need anything?' Flora asked.

'A get out of jail free card?'

'I could read my book to you. Though it is right at the end.'

'Don't bother.'

Sylvie stared at the ceiling. She heard Flora take out her book and settle on to the chair. Eventually, Mum arrived with an overnight bag.

Sylvie watched Mum unpack her washbag and nightie. She laid a dressing gown across the bottom of the bed. She'd even brought Teddy, though Sylvie was way too old for him to be seen in public. Sylvie shoved him under her pillow. Then she shifted the pillow a tiny bit, so that Teddy could still breathe.

'You don't have to stay, you know,' Mum said.

'I don't?' Sylvie sat up.

'No. If you want to give up on the trial and let me carry on helping you, you just have to say. Flora and I will come and get you any time,' Mum said.

'A plague on both your houses,' Sylvie muttered, and dropped back on to the bed.

'Don't quote Shakespeare at me,' Mum said. 'And don't forget to do your blood tests.' She dropped a kiss on to Sylvie's head. 'Come on, Flora, let's leave Sylvie to it.'

When they were gone, Sylvie stared up at the ceiling. A small crack spread across it like a fern. She would have to do a blood test every morning, lunchtime and evening. And take insulin every morning and evening. And remember to eat. That was it. Easy.

This was going to be a long, boring two days.

Then she heard the sounds on the ward change. Instead of clamour, there was cooing. Instead of wails, whispers. A ripple, a contagious murmur passing from child to child. What was it? Sylvie sat up. She could hear excited gasps, as though Santa had come to visit in the middle of summer.

Sylvie pulled back her curtain.

There, just next to the nurses' station, sat three dogs.

Dogs!

In hospital!

Were they sick?

There was a big yellow one who looked like a beanbag with a bacon rasher for a tongue – perhaps a Labrador? Beside that one, wagging its tail vigorously, was a white fluffy one. The third, with its head up and its eyes darting to take in everything, was a scruffy black-and-grey dog who looked like it was mid-shake, but wasn't – its fur just grew that way. It was, she thought, a dog of no particular breeding.

Sylvie noticed that in the bed beside hers, Caleb was struggling to sit up.

'Barry,' he said softly. 'Barry.'

The scruffiest dog pricked up his ears and thumped his tail hard on the ground.

'Barry,' Caleb said again.

The dog stood, wiggled the whole of the back half of his body and trotted over to Caleb's bed.

'Why is your dog here?' Sylvie asked. She leaned into the space between the beds, resting her hand on his cabinet.

Caleb sniffed. 'Barry isn't my dog. He's a therapy dog.'

'A what?'

Barry sat beside Caleb's bed, his tail still gently wagging, looking up with big, brown, adoring eyes. Caleb let his hand fall and Barry nudged his wet nose into Caleb's palm in a delighted greeting.

'The dogs are brought to cheer us up,' Caleb said.

'Oh.' Sylvie swung her feet down on to the floor and held her hand out towards Barry.

'No!' Caleb snapped. 'Barry is visiting me! You have to wait your turn.'

Sylvie snatched her hand back. 'Fine. I don't even want to say hello to that dog.'

Barry panted in her general direction, then licked Caleb's fingers.

'Yuck,' Sylvie said. 'It probably has germs too.'

She stuck out her tongue at Caleb, then stalked towards the nurses' station.

A small crowd had gathered around the two remaining dogs. Some children were stroking them, others watching from a wary distance.

Nurse Adams and a second nurse were trying to organise everyone. Sylvie thought the second nurse, a tall man with hair cut close to his scalp, might be called Nurse Ratchet or Hatchet – something like that. Nurse Adams was trying to get the children into some kind of order; Nurse Ratchet/Hatchet just glared.

'Everyone who wants to pat the dogs, please go to the day room,' Nurse Adams said. 'If you don't, then stay with Nurse Ratchet.' Ratchet, then.

'Day room. Now,' Nurse Ratchet growled.

Sylvie followed the swell of children, the two capering dogs and Nurse Adams into the day room. The day room was Peter Pan Ward at its most colourful. Mini tables and chairs, cushions and rugs in pinks and greens and reds. Books and toys and random-shaped plastic in a headache of colours. She sat on a beanbag and waited to see what happened. She wasn't patient – a patient, yes; patient, no – but she didn't want to seem desperate in front of the others. The Labrador sighed heavily as a small child flopped an arm around his huge tummy.

Eventually, Nurse Adams brought the white fluffy dog around to her. It still had a lot of energy, despite being rolled around and patted by half a dozen poorly children. It leaped up and rested its front paws on Sylvie's knee.

'This is Angus,' Nurse Adams said. 'He's a West Highland terrier.'

Angus grinned and licked Sylvie's kneecap. It tickled.

'Hello, Angus,' Sylvie whispered. There was something about his soft fur and grinning face that made the children's ward a little less horrible. She ruffled behind his ears and let her forehead drop on to the solid cube of his head.

'Help!'

She lifted her head. The cry had come from the ward.

'Help!' it came again. Anguished.

Angus barked and scurried out of the door. Nurse Adams was right behind him.

Sylvie was on her feet. Back towards the beds and the source of the shout – Caleb.

'It's Barry!' he said as soon as he saw Nurse Adams.

'What about him?' Nurse Adams looked at the ground, trying to see what was wrong with the scruffy dog. Sylvie looked too, but couldn't see him.

'He's gone!' Caleb said.

'What do you mean, gone? Did he leave the ward?'

'No,' Caleb said, his voice cracking with tears. 'He was here one minute, then gone the next. He's disappeared! Barry's disappeared!'

# Chapter Three

Caleb's already pale skin was tablet white. His fingers twitched at his sheets, tugging them higher and higher. He didn't get out of bed, despite the fact that his favourite dog had just vanished into thin air.

Why didn't he get up and rage about and yell? That's what Sylvie would have done. She'd have shouted until everyone in the hospital knew her dog was missing.

But he just lay there.

What exactly was wrong with him?

She opened her mouth to ask him, but Nurse Adams interrupted. 'I'm sure Barry's fine, wherever he is.'

'But where is he?' Caleb's voice was a high whine. 'He was right here. I closed my eyes for about a second. Then he was gone. I called and called. Where has he gone?'

Nurse Adams patted Caleb's white sheet as though it were a dog. 'Don't worry.'

Clip-clip-clip.

The sound of Nurse Ratchet heading over in his black boots sounded like a soldier marching. 'I hear we've temporarily lost a valuable item of medical equipment,' he said.

'A therapy dog, yes,' Nurse Adams replied.

'Well, not on my watch,' Nurse Ratchet said. 'He can't have left the ward.'

Sylvie liked Nurse Ratchet about as much as she liked wasps on a jam scone. But that didn't stop him being right. The dog couldn't have opened the main door, not without someone pressing the buzzer for him. He must still be here.

Sylvie dropped down and looked under Caleb's bed. Polished tiles and a stray sock. No dog. Beyond the bed, she could see Nurse Adams's sensible flat shoes, Nurse Ratchet's black boots, someone in panda slippers, a night-gown hem, some knobbly knees, the bottom of a tracksuit and bare feet – whoever that was would get a telling-off from the nurses – but no dog.

Still on all fours, she turned to look the other way. More feet now, as children filed out of the day room, curious to know what was wrong. Plus the scampering paws of Angus and the slow, steady plod of the Labrador.

'Children,' Nurse Ratchet barked, 'this ward is now divided into search zones. Your zone is your own bed. Please check your zone. You are searching for a lost item of equipment who answers to the name Barry.'

Sylvie got off the floor and dusted down her hands.

All around her children bustled towards their beds. Barry's name was called out, whispered and yelled.

But there was no sign of the dog.

Perhaps there was another way he could have got out?

She turned full circle, slowly, ignoring the bedlam. There! The emergency exit. Right next to the window. This was a mystery that had taken her thirty seconds to solve. She swaggered past Caleb's bed, past her own, past a confused-looking toddler and the empty final bed, then rested her hands on the door.

Someone must have leaned on the bar and Barry must have scuttled out, desperate to get away from bad-tempered Caleb. Simple.

She'd cracked it. Barry must have escaped down the outside stairs and was probably running around the car park causing havoc. She chuckled and played a little celebration drum roll on the bar with her fingers.

Oh. Her fingers had tapped something that scuppered her solution.

The bar was tagged. Hanging from it, like a dog's name from its collar, was a green plastic band. It was meant to snap easily if someone opened the door. If it was snapped, it told the staff that one of the children might have made a run for it. It wasn't snapped.

That green band meant one thing – this door hadn't been opened. Her solution to the mystery was wrong.

Rats.

Sylvie dropped her forehead on to the cool glass, letting its coldness soothe her. Behind her, the ward was up in arms – she could hear the rush and stomp of the search. But, for a moment, she just needed to hold herself still and quiet. This wasn't how she had planned on spending her day. She had thought that she would visit Dr Malcolm, persuade him that she should manage her own care, then meet her friends in the cafe on Marsh Road to celebrate. Instead she was stuck on a hospital ward where whole dogs could just – poof – disappear.

Her thoughts were interrupted – the way everything was on the children's ward – by a little person.

The little person tugged at her arm, pulling it away from the door.

Sylvie looked down. The little person was tiny, a

27

toddler, really, maybe three or four years old. She had blonde curls and blue eyes and the sort of angelic look that made Sylvie not trust her at all.

'*Bonjour,*' the little girl said.

French? Sylvie frowned. She'd been to France lots of times – Dad liked skiing – but she couldn't speak much of the language. Flora was better at it.

'Hello,' Sylvie said finally.

The girl sighed. 'Hello,' she said. 'What is going, please?'

'Sorry?'

'Why is it?' The girl waved a hand at the ward.

'Oh.' Sylvie realised the girl was asking why everyone was rushing about shouting. 'The dog has gone,' she said slowly. 'Everyone is looking for it.'

'Barry?' The girl pronounced it oddly – the 'ee' noise at the end went on for ages.

'Yes, exactly,' Sylvie replied.

'Yes. I seed him.'

'You saw?'

The blonde curls bobbed as the girl nodded.

Sylvie felt a jolt of excitement – maybe she could be the one to solve this mystery after all, with the help of a miniature French person. She dropped into a squat, so that her eyes were level with the girl's. It was important that the small person told her everything she knew. She should start with easy questions. 'What's your name?' Sylvie asked.

'Celine.'

'How old are you?'

'Four.'

So far so good. Now for something trickier. 'What did you see, Celine?'

Celine leaned in closely, so that Sylvie could smell her strawberry shampoo. The little girl's eyes were wide. She bit her lip before whispering, 'Barry, he was took by … by … I don't comprehend … by the Whiter.'

'The Whiter? What's the Whiter?'

'Hush!' Celine's eyes darted left and right, checking to see there was no one there. A shiver tingled its way up Sylvie's spine.

'The Whiter,' Celine insisted. 'In his sack.'

'The Whiter is a man? With a sack?' Sylvie scoffed. That didn't sound likely. A man with a sack stealing dogs in the middle of the day?

Celine nodded slowly. 'Don't be loud. He is listening.' Celine wrapped her arms tightly about herself, as though she were cold. But the children's ward was always boiling.

'Is it a person, or a machine, or …' Sylvie couldn't think what Celine might be trying to describe. It sounded like Evil Santa. '… or a robot?'

'Yes,' Celine replied.

Great.

'Is there anything else you can tell me?' Sylvie asked.

'I like trees,' Celine said.

Useless.

'What did he look like?' Sylvie asked.

Celine popped her thumb in her mouth.

'Celine!' Sylvie snapped.

Immediately, Celine's eyes swam with tears. Her chin shook.

'No!' Sylvie said. 'Don't cry. Stop!'

But there was no stopping Celine. She popped out her thumb and let out the biggest wail that Sylvie had ever heard. She covered her ears. Nurse Adams was there in a heartbeat, scooping up the child in her arms and making soothing noises. But it was no use. Celine's sobs were loud and snotty. Sylvie shuddered.

Toddlers made terrible witnesses.

The commotion hadn't gone unnoticed on the ward. Celine managed to squeeze out the word 'Whiter' between gasping heaves, and the word 'sack'.

A boy with his leg in a cast said that the Whiter was a ghost who ate children.

Another boy, with a rash on one cheek said that the Whiter was a dog snatcher who only appeared at night, and stood over you when you were sleeping.

A third boy claimed loudly that he too had seen the Whiter and that his hands were made of ice, frozen in claws.

Celine's sobs became screams.

'Hush, hush,' Nurse Adams said over the wails to the ward in general. 'There's no such thing as the Whiter. This is just fairy stories.'

'Quiet down, now!' Nurse Ratchet said. 'Or you'll all be sent to bed early.'

Nurse Adams carried the distraught Celine towards the nurses' station, where a big tin of chocolates helped to soothe most scrapes. The ward was hushed. But it was the frightened hush of children waiting for news. Where was Barry? Had he been taken by a ghost? A dog snatcher? An ice monster? Who would be next?

Sylvie stomped back to her bed and pulled the curtains closed. Mum had left her overnight bag beside the cabinet. Sylvie hoped that Mum had packed the one thing that she couldn't do without – her phone. Because whatever

31

was going on here needed more than just a tin of chocolates to sort it out.

She rifled through. Her fingers touched cold plastic. Yes!

In moments she was dialling Flora.

'Sylvie, what's up? Are you OK?'

'No,' Sylvie replied. 'Something is stalking the hospital,
and I don't mean Dr Malcolm in a bad mood. Something's up.'

'Like a mystery?' Flora asked.

'Like a mystery,' Sylvie agreed.

'I'll call the others,' Flora said. 'We'll be with you as
soon as we can.'

# Chapter Four

Sylvie hung up and flopped back on to her bed. She'd wanted to solve Barry's disappearance with no help from anyone, in seconds. But that wasn't going to work. It was time to admit that she needed the others. Which was very annoying. She sighed and plumped the pillow. It might have been her own mystery and she could have been the lead investigator. That would have impressed Mum and proved she was grown up enough to look after herself and do all her own testing.

Testing! Sylvie gasped. What time was it? She checked her watch. Nearly noon. She'd almost forgotten to do a blood test!

She'd remembered just in time, though. She dropped out of bed and went to wash her hands. The ward was quieter now. The threat of a ghostly apparition had sent everyone to their beds, or into huddled groups. She could see Celine with chocolate-smeared cheeks, smiling at Nurse Adams.

She scrubbed her hands in the patients' bathroom, then went back to her bed and took out her kit. A quick prick on the side of her finger with her lancer and she had a bead of blood. She squeezed it on to the testing strip and waited while the machine read the level of sugar in it. Four. Hmm, a teensy bit low, but she'd eat lunch soon and then it would rise. Not bad. She made a note in her book and cleared the used bits and bobs away.

She strolled over to Nurse Adams at the nurses' station. 'I'm going to need to eat soon,' Sylvie said.

Nurse Adams ruffled Celine's hair and grinned. 'Excellent management, Sylvie. The food trolley will be on its way.'

Sylvie didn't have long to wait. An orderly in a red uniform wheeled a big silver box on to the ward moments later. He read from a list, then handed out plates of food to each patient in turn. Everyone ate off their own table on their beds. That was another of the things Sylvie hated about hospital. Eating in bed felt wrong. But she sighed and got on with it. She had to prove to Dr Malcolm that she could be trusted.

She noticed that Caleb didn't touch his plate. He lay

still and silent, his eyes closed. He wouldn't get better if he didn't eat. She didn't bother telling him that though; he'd only snap at her.

Once lunch was over, Sylvie wandered back to the nurses' station. 'Has anyone seen Barry yet?' she asked Nurse Adams.

The nurse shook her head. 'Nurse Ratchet called Hospital Security, but there's no sign.'

'We can't have a dog loose in the wards,' Nurse Ratchet said, coming out of the small office behind the desk. 'It isn't hygienic,' he added.

Nurse Adams didn't say any more because, at that moment, Sylvie heard a small whimper coming from their side of the desk. A doglike whimper. She leaped up on tiptoes and pulled herself up to get a good view behind the station. Barry?

No.

Curled up around each other, looking very forlorn, were Angus and the Labrador.

'We're not letting them out of our sight,' Nurse Ratchet said. 'Not until their handler comes to collect them.'

'When will that be?' Sylvie asked. An idea was beginning to form.

'Any minute. I've been calling them to collect these

two since Barry scarpered. They're better off out of here. We don't need the paperwork.'

'Please can I borrow Angus?' Sylvie asked.

'What? No. Those dogs are staying put.'

'Please? I just want to walk him on the ward, to see if he picks up Barry's scent. Angus might be able to find Barry straightaway!'

Nurse Ratchet exchanged a look with Nurse Adams, then shrugged. 'All right. But if another dog goes missing, you're filling in the forms.'

Sylvie took Angus's lead from Nurse Adams. She had a moment's wobble when she realised that she had no idea how to ask Angus to hunt. But then she just decided to explain his mission in the same way a director would talk to actors – ask for what she wanted.

'Angus,' she said brightly, 'find Barry!'

Angus's stumpy white tail whipped from side to side. Then he shot off, pulling Sylvie along behind like a water-skier. He scampered towards the day room. His nose was down, pressed close to the floor. Sylvie imagined a whole database of scents were whizzing up his nose, telling him exactly where Barry had gone. She clung to the lead.

Angus rounded the corner, his legs sliding out from underneath him.

Where was Barry?

Sylvie scanned the day room.

A boy in front of a jigsaw, something in his hand. A girl holding a plastic stethoscope to a doll's chest. No Barry.

Angus sniffed again. Then he launched himself at the boy, landing heavily in his lap. The boy yelped and raised his arms, protecting whatever it was he was holding.

Sylvie saw what it was, and sighed. 'Angus, that is not Barry, it's a butty. Two completely different things.'

Angus whined. The boy fed him a bit of crust.

Sylvie tugged on the lead and Angus leaped down from his perch. They headed back to the nurses' station, Angus delighted with his sandwich, Sylvie deciding she didn't like dogs very much.

'Visitors for you,' Nurse Ratchet said.

Sylvie raised her head. Standing by the main door were Flora, Piotr, Minnie and Andrew. She shoved Angus's lead back towards Nurse Adams, who took it with a smile. Had they seen Angus's rubbish attempt at search and rescue? She hoped not.

'Sylvie,' Piotr said, walking towards her, 'are you OK? We didn't know you were going into hospital.'

She felt the heat in her cheeks rise. Then she felt

embarrassed for being embarrassed. 'Yes, well, it's no big deal,' she snapped. 'I'm just here to prove I can take care of myself.'

'And have you?' Flora folded her arms. 'Have you done a blood test yet?'

'Yes. Stop nagging!'

'I wasn't.'

'You were.'

'Stop arguing,' Minnie said, 'and tell us why we're here.'

Sylvie gave a dramatic sigh, then waved them over to her bed. Usually, whenever they had a mystery to solve, the gang would meet at the market cafe or Minnie's mum's hair salon to talk it over, but right now they were stuck with floor-to-ceiling Disney princesses. Sylvie scooched up to the top of the bed. Flora and Minnie sat in the space she'd made. Andrew took the chair. Piotr stayed standing. It was a tight squeeze, but Sylvie had to admit to being pleased they'd come to help.

'Tell us what's happened,' Piotr said, taking charge.

Flora unzipped her backpack and fished out her investigator's notebook. Sylvie told them everything that had happened on the ward, from Caleb to Celine, while Flora scribbled furiously.

'So,' Andrew said when she'd finished, 'this kid says she saw something called the Whiter take the dog?'

Sylvie nodded. 'But she's only a baby, and can't really tell us what she saw. And her English isn't very good.'

'Is it a ghost, do you think? Or magic?'

'Andrew,' Sylvie said crushingly, 'there's no such thing as magic.'

'I'm ninety-five per cent certain that there's no such thing as magic,' Andrew said, 'but that still means there's a five per cent chance it's real.'

'No, it doesn't,' Minnie said. 'What do you know about Celine?'

Sylvie shrugged. She had no idea how a French toddler had ended up in the hospital ward. 'I think she's on holiday, or something.'

'What about spontaneous combustion?' Andrew said. 'Maybe the dog just burst into flames and was gone.'

'No ash, or smoke,' Sylvie said. 'I think we can be pretty sure it wasn't spontaneous combustion.'

'Mostly because that's not real either,' Flora added.

'Did anyone else see anything suspicious today?' Piotr asked.

Sylvie twisted strands of her red hair about her fingers. Had anyone else seen anything? Lots of kids had talked about seeing the Whiter, but only after Celine had mentioned it – she thought they were probably just imagining things. Everything else had been quite normal. There had only been that man, earlier …

'Wait!' she said. 'Me! I saw something suspicious. And Flora! We both did. Before I came on to the ward we saw a man with a bleeding hand, but he was running away from Minor Injuries, not towards it. In fact, he ran out of the hospital with a really bad cut. That's suspicious, isn't it?'

Flora's pencil hovered above her notebook as she wondered whether the man was worth recording. She decided he was, and her pencil returned to the page and picked up pace. Andrew's eyes were wide behind his glasses, and even Minnie managed to look a bit interested. Sylvie felt a rush of glee at Minnie's reaction. She and Minnie were friends … but not best friends, so for Minnie to listen felt like winning.

Piotr nodded. 'It does sound suspicious. Do you know where he was coming from?'

'He passed us on the stairs,' Sylvie said.

'Are you allowed off the ward? To show us?'

'I think so. Let's find out.'

She knew it was a bad idea to ask Nurse Ratchet, he

would just say no. But Nurse Adams might let her leave for a while.

'I just need to stretch my legs,' Sylvie explained a few moments later, 'perhaps get something from the cafe with my friends.'

Nurse Adams, who had the Labrador's head in her lap and was patting it distractedly, said, 'You won't leave the hospital, will you?'

'Of course not.'

'You promise?'

Sylvie thought good thoughts, pure, trustworthy, angelic thoughts. Then smiled. 'I promise.'

The side of Nurse Adams's mouth twitched. 'Fine. But be back in half an hour, tops. No one else is to go missing on my watch.'

Yes!

She managed to suppress her squeal until she was back behind the curtain with the others. Then she did a happy dance, arms to the side. Only Andrew joined in.

'Right,' she said, 'let's find the bleeding man.'

# Chapter Five

Sylvie and Flora, who knew the hospital better than the others, led the way back to the stairwell where they had seen the bleeding man.

Minnie walked at the back of the group, beside Andrew, with Piotr in the middle. 'Hey, Sylvie,' she called, 'what makes you so sure this man had anything to do with Barry going missing?'

The shout echoed down the bright corridor, bouncing off polished tiles and clean walls.

Sylvie looked back over her shoulder but didn't stop walking. 'I didn't say I was sure. Piotr asked if I'd seen anything suspicious. And the man was suspicious. That's all.'

Minnie folded her arms. 'I don't see what it has to do with the dog, though.'

Sylvie pressed her lips together tightly. Was Minnie trying to be irritating?

'It's good to check it out,' Piotr said.

'It's better than trying to find a ghost,' Sylvie added.

Andrew grinned. 'The Whiter! Wooooo!' He waved his arms in the air and raced to the front.

Piotr and Andrew always did their best to keep everyone smiling. Sylvie knew why she was friends with them. She wasn't always sure why they were friends with Minnie. Perhaps just because they'd known each other since nursery. Like her and Flora, they'd just found themselves together and it had been that way ever since.

They stopped when they came to the stairwell. A few people had passed them in the corridor, staff and visitors, as well as the occasional patient. But the hospital felt more like a hotel than a place full of sick people – nice paintings on the walls and leafy green plants were meant to distract attention from the smell of disinfectant and sickness. It worked. Mostly. The stairwell was light and the banister was so smooth and polished that holding it was like holding a friend's hand.

There was no sign of the man now, but Sylvie hadn't really expected to see him.

'He came from upstairs,' Flora said. 'We were leaving Dr Malcolm's office, so he had to be coming from the top floor.'

They went up two flights of stairs to the top of the hospital. Up here the quiet was almost serene. Sylvie hadn't been here before. There were no signs for wards – instead, the royal-blue plaques said things like 'Human Resources' and 'Data Management', apart from one yellow sign that said 'Wet Floor'.

'It's the space for the hospital's office staff,' Piotr said.

'Which room did he come from?' Sylvie wondered aloud.

Flora cocked her head to one side, thinking. 'When you cut yourself it bleeds most in the first few seconds. That's when it drips, before it's had a chance to coagulate.'

'Coagulate?' Andrew asked.

'Scab over,' Flora explained. 'And if it dripped on to the floor ...'

'Then someone would mop it up!' Andrew finished.

They headed to the 'Wet Floor' sign.

The floor was dry – whoever had mopped it had done it a while ago. The sign was outside an office with 'Heather Black: Human Resources' written on the door.

'Sounds weird,' Andrew said, 'like she might have body parts for Frankenstein in there.'

'Sorry, Andrew, it just means the people who interview staff for jobs,' Flora said.

They paused outside the door, not sure what to do next. Then Minnie raised her fist and knocked.

'Come in!' a lady's voice said.

Minnie pushed the door open, but Sylvie managed to duck inside first. There was enough room for them all inside. It was an office, about the same size as Dr Malcolm's on the floor below. Afternoon sunlight spilled like treacle on to the pale yellow walls. A neat woman, presumably Heather Black, sat behind an even neater desk. Heather smiled, a little uncertainly, at the troop of children standing in her office.

'Can I help you? Are you lost?' she asked. Her voice was like treacle too, warm and sweet.

Andrew stepped forward. 'Hello. We're the Marsh Road Investigators. You might have heard of us?'

Heather raised the corner of her mouth, but said nothing.

'We investigate mysteries wherever we find them,' Andrew said. 'And we have been lucky enough to find one here. The Mystery of the Disappearing Dog. The Case of the Pinched Pup. The ...'

'The Riddle of the Vamoosed Varmint?' Minnie suggested.

'Hey, that's really good!' Andrew said.

Heather gave a discreet cough.

'Sorry,' Andrew continued. 'A dog has gone missing on the children's ward and we are looking for it. We heard that there was a man, acting suspiciously, in this part of the building earlier on today and we hoped you might know more.'

Heather laid her elbows on her desk and tapped her pale peach nails together. 'You must mean the man from Maintenance.'

'What did he look like?' Piotr asked.

Heather's eyebrows furrowed as she tried to remember. 'Tallish, dark hair, I think. He was wearing a cap. It was the strangest thing,' Heather said. 'He told me that he had been sent to fix the radiator in here. But there's nothing wrong with it. And, anyway, it's summer – it doesn't even need to be on. But he said it had to be done; he showed me the work order, so I let him. The next thing I knew, he had cut himself on something. It looked quite bad. There's no first-aid kit in here. The nearest one is in Payroll, three doors down. I went to get it – I make sure that all staff have basic first-aid training, not just the medics – anyway, by the time I came back, the man was gone. I assume he went to find a trained doctor.'

Sylvie and Flora exchanged a look – they knew he hadn't done that at all!

'Why wouldn't he wait for the first-aid kit?' Minnie asked.

Sylvie had no answer.

Piotr wandered towards the window. The view was of a few lime lollipop trees, the cars in the car park and some green storage buildings beyond. One of the buildings was daubed in rainbow graffiti. Above, a seagull whirled over the tarmac, eyeing the ground for dropped crisps.

'What if …' Piotr said slowly. 'What if he cut himself deliberately?'

'Why would anyone do that?' Andrew asked.

Sylvie raised an eyebrow at Andrew – he must have forgotten that she deliberately cut her finger every day! He missed the look entirely.

'I mean,' Piotr explained, 'if the man wanted this office to himself for a few minutes, then forcing you to get the first-aid kit is a great way to make that happen.'

Heather frowned. 'He wanted me gone?'

'It's a good hypothesis,' Flora said, 'until anyone can suggest anything better. So, the question is, what is there in this room that someone might want?'

Heather chuckled. 'There's nothing valuable in here. No safe. None of the good Dame Julie Dent paintings. Not even a stash of high quality chocolate biscuits! No, the only thing in here are the staff employment records.'

'Could anyone want those?' Flora asked.

There was a flicker of anxiety across Heather's face. 'No, I shouldn't think so.' Then a look of worry. 'I mean, no, definitely not.' Then a look of panic. 'I'll just check the files.'

She tapped at her keyboard and watched the screen, her eyes darting up and down, searching for something.

She gasped when she found it.

'There was activity on the filing system at 11.17 a.m., but I wasn't using the files this morning,' she said.

'When was the man here?'

'I'd just finished drinking my eleven o'clock coffee,' Heather whispered.

Sylvie could have done Andrew's victory dance! She'd known the man was suspicious! And here was the proof! She didn't know yet how it fitted in with Barry's disappearance, but she bet it did. 'See?' she said to Minnie.

She was about to add, 'I told you so,' when Piotr butted in.

'Can you tell what he did, while he was on the system?' Piotr said.

Heather bit her lip. 'I can't. I'm not that good with technology. I bet someone from IT will know, though. I feel so stupid.' She hung her head and her hair fell over her face.

Minnie reached across the desk and patted Heather on her shoulder. 'It wasn't your fault; you were trying to be kind.'

Heather's shaking hand reached for the phone. 'I have to call IT. They need to look at my computer.'

'And we need to find Barry,' Andrew said. 'Thanks to you, we now have a suspect.'

# Chapter Six

'We can't be sure that Barry going missing and this man using the computer are linked,' Minnie said, moments later. 'It might just be a coincidence.'

They were outside Heather's office, sitting on the top few stairs. Flora was writing everything down in her notebook, while the others thought about what Minnie had said.

'It would be a big coincidence,' Andrew said, 'if there were two weird things happening in the same morning. Also, no one would suspect someone from Maintenance – they must be able to go wherever they like in the hospital without anyone paying any attention. It's the perfect camouflage. I think the man used the computer, then stole the dog somehow. We're looking for a member of staff.'

'But why kidnap the dog?' Piotr said. 'What for?'

'Perhaps he didn't kidnap the dog,' Andrew suggested.

'Maybe he used the computer to build a portal through space and time and the dog accidentally got sucked through the rip in the universe?'

Flora laughed. 'If that really is the solution to the mystery, then I'll buy you your own body weight in cream cakes at the cafe.'

Andrew nudged her gently with his shoulder. 'You never know,' he said.

Flora underscored something in her notebook, then closed it. 'It's not clear yet how, or if, the two events are connected. Was there any sign of this maintenance man on the children's ward, Sylvie?'

'No, the only thing anyone saw was Celine's weird Whiter.'

Creases appeared between Piotr's eyebrows. 'Yes. What was she trying to say? I can't think of anything.'

Sylvie brought her feet together so that the heels of her shoes clicked. She hated staying in the hospital, but at least this time it was a lot more interesting than usual. 'What next?' she asked the others.

'Sylvie,' Flora said carefully, 'how long have you been away from the ward?'

Urgh! Sylvie gave a dramatic shiver. Why did Flora have to bring that up? 'Not long,' she said firmly.

'Nurse Adams gave you half an hour.'

'It hasn't been anywhere near half an hour,' Sylvie said. She knew it had been at least half an hour. Nurse Adams wasn't her mum, though. She had just said half an hour because that was the first number that had popped into her head. It hadn't been for any particular reason. And Sylvie hated doing things for no reason.

Flora was staring at her.

'Look,' Sylvie said, 'I'll go back in a minute. I just want to check out Maintenance first. What if Barry's there right now? Nurse Adams would want me to follow this lead.'

'Nurse Adams would want you to do what you were told,' Flora said.

'And I will,' Sylvie said. 'After we've been to Maintenance.'

The maintenance office wasn't somewhere that Sylvie went to regularly, but she had half an idea where it was: on the ground floor of the hospital, behind the cafe and kitchens. Like the children's ward, this section of the hospital had a buzzer to open the door. But, unlike the children's ward, there were catering staff and cleaners and orderlies and delivery drivers coming and going through the door constantly. Andrew waited until someone used their badge to open the door, then ducked through behind them. Once inside, he held the door open and waved the others in.

The staff side of the hospital wasn't as nicely decorated as the public areas. The floor was laid with lino instead of tiles. The walls were all one shade of magnolia, rather than the array of soft pastels that made the public areas feel like a hotel. But it was all ruthlessly clean and well cared for.

'Try to look like you're meant to be here,' Andrew said softly.

Sylvie knew that all you had to do to stay under the radar was to look as though you belonged. Though why anyone would believe that five children had any business on the staff side of the hospital wasn't exactly clear. Still. She thought *belonging, belonging, belonging* as hard as she could, and followed the others with her head held high.

The corridor smelled of the cafe kitchens: a mixture of too many foods to be tasty – damp vegetables, frying oils, baked sugar and the fatty, greasy tang of gravy on everything. The area was alive with sounds too, pots clanking and clattering at the wash-up, shouted instructions, doors opening and closing. They walked quickly past the hot and humid space.

Maintenance wasn't any quieter. Hammering sounds and an electric drill thumped and whizzed in the air. The noises were muffled by a big blue door, with 'Authorised Personnel Only' written on it.

'What should we do?' Flora asked doubtfully.

'Well,' Minnie said, 'we don't want to go inside, we just want to talk to whoever's in there. So I say we just knock.'

For once, Sylvie agreed with Minnie, so she knocked loudly on the door. The sound of drilling stopped. The door was opened moments later by a gruff-looking man with grey hair in his red beard. 'Yes?' he said.

'We're looking for someone,' Sylvie said.

'Aren't we all,' the man replied. Which Sylvie thought was a very odd thing to say.

'A specific someone,' Flora added.

The door opened a little wider. Sylvie could make out the benches and tools of a workshop. The man in the doorway blocked much of the view, as he was quite wide; his blue overalls stretched at the seams. But there was someone else in there too, holding a hammer; she was wearing the same overalls and her face was streaked with sweat.

'What sort of specific someone?' the man asked.

'Someone from Maintenance,' Piotr said.

'Me or Cheryl?' the man replied.

'Neither. The tall man with dark hair,' Sylvie said.

The man in the doorway looked over his shoulder at the woman with the hammer. She shrugged at him. 'There's no tall man,' he said, looking back at them, 'it's just us two that work here.'

'Are you sure?'

'Of course I'm sure.'

Andrew stepped forward. 'There's a dog who has disappeared from the children's ward. He didn't go out of the door. Are there any other ways out? Like ventilation shafts? Or secret tunnels? Or anything like that?'

The man grinned and rubbed his beard. 'Secret tunnels, eh? No, there's none of them in this hospital. Ventilation, yes, but those tubes are no wider than a drainpipe. I always laugh in spy films when people crawl down them – only a pencil could fit down them in real life. No, sorry, son, I can't help you there.'

The man waited a second to see if anyone else would speak. When no one did, he closed the door. Seconds later the hammering and drilling started again, but the investigators were silent.

* * *

Sylvie scuffed her shoes against the floor, dragging her heels as they headed back out to the atrium. She was going to be in trouble with Nurse Adams for being late. And with Dr Malcolm for not displaying adequate levels of being a responsible sort of person. And for nothing. Their lead led nowhere.

'So,' Andrew said, 'my rip in space-time theory is still the main contender!'

Sylvie forced a smile. Andrew was a fool sometimes, but he was *their* fool.

They were back in the public area now, and the yells and clatters of people going about hospital business were giving Sylvie a headache.

'We need to consider the facts,' Flora said. She stopped briefly by a bench and pulled out her notebook. She flipped it open, then realised that there was a security guard standing nearby, so she kept on walking. When she spoke, her voice was just a whisper. 'Here's where we stand. Stop me if I miss anything out. At 11.20-ish this morning, Sylvie and I see an injured man, wearing what appears to be a maintenance uniform, running away from the hospital. Neither of us get a good look at his face, but we know he was tall, with dark hair. Then, at 11.45-ish, therapy dog Barry disappears from the children's ward. The only witness is a toddler who says "the Whiter" took him. A search of the children's ward found no clue as to the dog's whereabouts. Tracing the injured man led us to Heather, who discovered that the employee files had been accessed earlier that day by the injured man.' She looked up and closed her notebook. 'That man doesn't work in Maintenance.'

'But he probably works at the hospital!' Andrew said suddenly. 'He was accessing the employee files. He had the right paperwork to convince Heather he was meant to be there, and he had the right uniform. And if he did steal Barry, then he would have needed a staff pass to get on to the children's ward without needing to be buzzed in. All those things would be easy if he were a member of staff.' Andrew glanced suspiciously around the busy foyer – any one of the doctors, nurses, guards, cleaners or receptionists might be guilty!

'You might be right,' Piotr said. 'So, we're looking for a tall, dark man who has easy access to the children's ward in order to kidnap a dog. And a cut on his hand.'

There was one name that immediately popped into Sylvie's head.

# Chapter Seven

'Dr Malcolm!' Sylvie said. 'He's tall and dark and he has access to the ward!' She picked up her pace, pounding up the stairs.

'Sylvie!' Flora shouted after her. 'You have to go back to the ward. Nurse Adams!'

Sylvie slowed. She stopped. Flora was right. She was already fifteen minutes late and she was supposed to be proving how sensible she could be. But what if Dr Malcolm had Barry? But what if Mum decided she hadn't been grown up enough? 'Fine!' Sylvie yelled. Then stomped towards the ward. The others raced behind her.

Flora caught up. 'One of us can interview Dr Malcolm while you check back in on the ward.'

What? She was going to get shoved out of the way with the silly little kids while they had all the fun? 'No way! You've got to wait for me.'

'Sylvie.' Piotr had caught up with them now. His voice was gentle, kind. 'Sylvie, think about Barry. He needs us to look for him. It doesn't matter which of us interviews Dr Malcolm, as long as one of us does.'

It did matter! It had been her idea. Her suggestion. It wasn't fair. 'I hate this place!' she said finally, and pressed the buzzer, hard, outside the children's ward.

'We'll come in with you,' Piotr said softly. 'Me and Minnie. Flora and Andrew can go and look for the doctor.'

Sylvie didn't look at him. She could feel rosy spots of indignation burning her cheeks. At least Minnie wasn't getting to do her job.

The door clicked open. She gave it a hard shove. 'Nurse Adams, I'm back!' she shouted.

At the nurses' station, Nurse Adams frowned and checked her watch. 'You're late,' she said doubtfully. 'Where have you been?'

Sylvie was about to yell at Nurse Adams too, when she felt Piotr's hand on her arm, warm and friendly. He cared about her. Even if everyone else was a pain. She gave him a tight smile.

'Well?' Nurse Adams asked.

Sylvie's smile grew. 'Nurse Adams,' she said, 'in peace

there's nothing so becomes a girl as modest stillness and humility: but – and this is the important bit – when the blast of war blows in our ears, then that girl must imitate the action of a tiger!'

'Sorry?'

'It's from a play. I've been looking for Barry. I've been imitating the actions of a tiger.'

'Well,' Nurse Adams said, 'that's as maybe. But tigers should learn to tell the time.'

Flora and Andrew went back to the stairwell and climbed up, towards Dr Malcolm's office.

'I know Dr Malcolm has a pass to get on to Peter Pan Ward,' Flora said, 'but did he have the opportunity? I mean, Sylvie and I sat outside his office for twenty minutes while the maintenance man was in Heather's office and we didn't see Dr Malcolm go in or out. And what about motive? Why would he steal a dog?'

'Maybe he's doing experiments and he needs a dog to do them on, like the dog they sent into space,' Andrew suggested. 'Or maybe he's after a clever dog to do talent shows with, or perhaps he's secretly going blind and wants to train a dog to guide him?'

'Well, at least we can always rely on your imagination,' Flora said.

They had reached the polished wooden door of Dr Malcolm's office. They could see their own fuzzy reflections in the varnish. 'How do we handle this?' Andrew asked, sounding slightly shaky. He'd had a lot to do with doctors when his mum was ill, Flora knew. Perhaps he didn't like the idea of a doctor being a dog thief? Or perhaps he was just intimidated by people in white coats.

'Don't worry,' she told him. 'I'm sure it will be all right.'

She rapped smartly on the door and waited for the dignified, patrician 'Come in,' before pushing it open.

'Ah, Sylvie Hampshire,' Dr Malcolm said. 'Back again. What's the matter?'

'No, not Sylvie. I'm Flora. And this is my friend Andrew.' Flora walked purposefully across the room and sat down opposite Dr Malcolm. Andrew dragged a chair from the back wall. Its squeal as it moved across the tiled floor made everyone wince.

'Delighted, I'm sure,' Dr Malcolm said uncertainly. His hands rested on his lap, below the line of the desk. She couldn't see them, let alone any scab or cut.

61

'Shake hands, Andrew,' Flora said as brightly as she could manage.

Andrew leaped up out of his chair and jabbed his right hand out. Dr Malcolm's face was a mask of confusion, but he reached out anyway. His hand was wrapped tight inside a surgical glove. Andrew grabbed it and, before Dr Malcolm could protest, had turned it over, and back again, eyeing the skin that looked plastic and yellow beneath the glove.

Dr Malcolm snatched back his hand. 'Sit!' he told Andrew.

Andrew sat.

'Wow!' Flora said. 'You said that like a dog trainer. You should be on telly teaching people how to get their new puppy to behave. Are you good with dogs?'

'What?' Dr Malcolm's bafflement increased – his waggling eyebrows seemed to be dancing a rumba.

'Dogs,' Flora said simply. 'Do you like them?'

'No, not really,' Dr Malcolm said. 'What can I do for you two? Do you have questions about your sister's trial?'

Flora shook her head. 'It's the children's ward. Is Sylvie safe there, do you think?'

'Safe?' Dr Malcolm goggled.

'Yes. Have you heard about the dog disappearing?'

Dr Malcolm pressed his fingertips together. She could see dark hairs squished flat by the gloves, but no sign of a cut, or a plaster. 'I'm sure your sister is perfectly safe.'

'Do you know anything about the dog? Perhaps you were on the ward? Did you see anything? If I knew what happened, I'd feel much better about my sister staying there.'

'I was not on the ward, no.' Dr Malcolm picked up an expensive-looking pen and began to doodle on his pad. He drew a cake. 'I haven't been on the ward at all today. I've been seeing patients in the holistic health centre. The slimmers' club. It's made me think about snacks all morning,' Dr Malcolm replied, adding candles to his doodled cake. 'My rounds are scheduled for this after-noon. Though I may pop down sooner. Someone has been spreading rumours about a monster living under the beds. Some of the little ones are quite frightened.'

'The Whiter?' Andrew suggested.

'Some such silly name, yes. We need to nip this nonsense in the bud. Right after snack time. In fact, if there's nothing you need from me, I'm going to visit the cafe.'

Andrew stood up. 'It's been lovely to meet you, Doctor.' He thrust out his left hand.

Dr Malcolm raised one eyebrow and pointedly slipped both hands into the pockets of his white coat.

They were being dismissed.

Flora stood, reluctantly. 'Maybe there is some kind of gremlin or poltergeist about,' she said, watching Dr Malcolm's face closely. 'I heard that someone in the offices had their computer files tampered with by a strange visitor earlier today.'

Dr Malcolm's face didn't flicker. It had the stony stillness of a garden wall. 'Really, Flora,' he said, 'you shouldn't spread these silly stories. It frightens the little ones.' There was no sign of a blush, or a twitch, or a tell of any kind. If he had touched Heather's computer, then he was a better actor than Sylvie.

'And,' he added, 'I think your mother would prefer it if you didn't investigate the missing dog. I assume that is what you're doing? I have heard about your exploits in the past. Sylvie is here to prove to your parents that she can be responsible. Don't encourage her to get distracted by a wild goose chase.'

'It isn't a wild goose,' Andrew said, 'it's a lost dog.'

'Either way –' Was it her imagination, or did Dr

Malcolm sound a tiny bit menacing? 'Either way, stay out of it. Leave it to the professionals.'

As she left the office, Flora wondered whether Dr Malcolm had meant for that to sound like a threat.

# Chapter Eight

Sylvie, Piotr and Minnie were in the day room. Sylvie flicked jigsaw pieces into the open neck of a doll without a head. 'It's not fair,' she said. 'Flora should have come back to the ward and pretended to be me so that I could go and interview Dr Malcolm. I'd have made her, if I'd thought of it in time.'

Minnie, who had her long legs stretched out on the floor and her head rested against a beanbag, gave a short laugh. 'Yeah, that would really prove to everyone how mature you are.'

Sylvie flicked a piece a bit too hard. It bounced off the doll and dropped down the side of a toy box.

'She'll let us know how it goes,' Piotr said.

'Dr Malcolm can't be the only doctor who has access to the children's ward anyway,' Minnie said.

'No,' Sylvie replied. 'But most of the doctors who

work on the children's ward are ladies. I've noticed it before. Most of the nurses are too. It's only Nurse Ratchet who's a man.' Her hand stilled, the jigsaw piece hovering like an unflipped coin. 'Hey! Nurse Ratchet! He's got dark hair. And he's pretty tall.'

She was on fire! That was two suspects she'd identified for the gang. Knowing the hospital was turning out to be quite a good thing after all.

Minnie rose up on to her elbow. The beans inside the bag hissed as she moved. 'Why would Nurse Ratchet steal a dog?'

'He doesn't like dogs,' Sylvie said. 'He thinks they're unhygienic. And I have to say, he has a point.'

Piotr got up off the tiny red chair he'd been sitting on. 'Well,' he said, 'if you have to be here, we might as well make use of it. Let's go and find out what he knows.'

The sound of the ward was still a little subdued, as though an invisible mist had crept in and muffled the noise. Or maybe it was the children themselves who were subdued, worried that a creature who could appear from nowhere and take Barry might leap from the shadows and take them too. If they were small, and quiet, and still, perhaps the Whiter might not turn his eye on them.

Nurse Ratchet was standing in front of an open linen closet, staring at neat piles of folded white sheets. He was ticking off a list on his clipboard. His badge hung off the board on a lanyard and Sylvie could see his awful photo, a mugshot that made him look like a criminal. Was he one?

'Hello,' Sylvie said.

Nurse Ratchet startled. 'You made me jump. Do you need something?'

Sylvie looked hard at Nurse Ratchet before answering. His pale face had the barest hint of dark stubble on his chin. His pastel-blue uniform was immaculate, pressed to within an inch of its life. His arms were bare. His hands? From where she was standing, his hands were clean, with neatly trimmed nails, and no sign at all of a cut.

'Do you know anything about dogs?' she asked. 'I mean, do you have a dog at home?'

Nurse Ratchet shook his head swiftly. 'Not likely. Shedding hair everywhere. Sniffing in all kinds of unpleasant places.'

Sylvie nodded sagely. 'Yes, if we had a dog, we'd go through litres of hand sanitiser. I wouldn't mind, but that stuff stings if it gets into a cut, don't you find? Do your hands sting right now?'

Nurse Ratchet's nose wrinkled in confusion. Then he cast a suspicious glance at Minnie. She had moved up close behind him and was staring at his hands. He folded his arms, tucking his hands out of view.

'Did you see anything suspicious earlier?' Piotr asked. 'When Barry disappeared?'

Nurse Ratchet shrugged. 'You mean apart from the dogs being on the ward in the first place? No. I was in the office on the computer. I didn't see a thing.' Nurse Ratchet slid his right hand up his face to stroke his chin. His fingers were thin, and strong-looking, like a pianist's. There was no sign of an injury.

It looked as though Nurse Ratchet was innocent – or at least wasn't the man who had cut himself in Heather's office.

'Something peculiar happened in the Human Resources office too this morning,' Piotr said. 'Do you know anything about that?'

Nurse Ratchet glanced up at the ceiling, as though seeking strength. 'I started work at seven this morning,' he said. 'What with all the commotion I've not even had time to eat a cheese roll yet, let alone go wandering about the hospital talking to office staff. Some of us have real jobs to do!'

At that moment, the door buzzer sounded. And again. And again. Like a hornet in a teapot, it buzzed loudly and angrily.

Someone was waiting outside the children's ward. And whoever it was, was in an absolutely terrible mood.

# Chapter Nine

The buzzer sounded once more. A long, drawn-out rattle, as whoever was outside held their finger down on it.

'What on earth?' Nurse Ratchet snapped. He stomped over to the nurses' station, grabbed the white telephone receiver and barked into it. 'Yes?'

The reply sounded like a hornet buzzing too – crashing into the mouth of the receiver.

Nurse Ratchet's face became a shade or two paler. 'Oh. Yes, sir,' he said, 'one moment.' He pressed the door release button. The gang swivelled on their heels to see who it was that could make one of the grumpiest nurses quake in his sensible boots.

The ward door banged open, the handle crunching against the plaster on the wall. A man barrelled in. He was huge, tall and wide with muscle. His dark suit was the same shade as his hair. 'Caleb!' he yelled, his voice deep like thunder on a mountaintop. 'Caleb!'

He stalked across the floor, completely ignoring the gang and Nurse Ratchet.

'Sir!' Nurse Ratchet called.

The man held up a firm hand – *no*. He didn't even look Nurse Ratchet's way.

'Caleb.' His voice was softer now, as he saw the boy lying listless in his bed.

'Who's he?' Sylvie whispered in her softest voice.

She got her answer straightaway.

'How are you doing, son?' the man said. Caleb's dad. Mr Burroughs.

Mr Burroughs asked his son a few questions, leaning in close to catch the faint replies, then he stormed over to the nurses' station. His round face was mottled strawberry. His cheeks puffed out and the veins at his neck and temple were thick vines below his skin. 'You lost that dog!' he growled.

'The animal is temporarily misplaced,' Nurse Ratchet said frostily.

'Where is it?' Mr Burroughs bellowed.

'Misplaced means I don't know.'

'I know what misplaced means! What I don't know is how you bunch of spring showers managed to lose a living, breathing creature from your care. Were you asleep? Chatting about last night's telly? Were you, in fact, being totally incompetent?'

Nurse Ratchet dropped his hands on to the desk with a smack. 'I resent your implications!' he said.

Sylvie, Piotr and Minnie, still near the linen cupboard, listened intently.

'These are not implications!' Mr Burroughs was yelling now. 'They are out and out accusations! If you lose a dog, what's to say it won't be a child next time?'

From a bed near the nurses' station, a child began wailing.

'You're upsetting the patients!' Nurse Ratchet snapped.

'They should be upset! Their safety has been compromised. You can be darn sure that every news outlet in a fifty-mile radius is going to hear about this security breach. Our children aren't safe with you!'

'Lower your voice.'

'I will not!'

'You will!'

'Won't.'

'I'm calling security.' Nurse Ratchet reached for the phone.

'Dad!' Caleb's voice was weak. 'Dad!' he tried again.

But it was no use. Mr Burroughs and Nurse Ratchet were squabbling over the phone. Both had their hands on the receiver, tugging it back and forth like toddlers fighting over a toy truck.

Sylvie turned her back on the adults. She nodded to Piotr and Minnie to follow. She stopped at the foot of Caleb's bed. She was shocked by how pale he was – like a drawing left out in sunlight, his lines and edges seemed to be fading.

'Are you OK?' Minnie asked.

'I wish he wasn't shouting,' Caleb said.

Piotr, who knew about protective parents, said, 'He's just worried about you.'

'I know. But yelling doesn't solve anything. It won't bring Barry back.'

'We're looking for him, you know,' Sylvie said.

Caleb's dark eyes, set with shadows, turned fully on Minnie's face. They were alight with hope. Then that light was crushed out. 'What difference will that make?' Caleb said scornfully.

'We're good at solving mysteries,' Minnie said. 'We've done it before.'

Caleb pulled his sheet higher, his thin fingers pressed against his chin. 'Do you know where he is, then?'

'Not yet.'

Caleb pulled the sheet right over his head. Sylvie thought she could just detect a faint trembling in his shoulders – was he crying?

'We'll keep looking,' she said.

'Leave me alone.' The reply was muffled by the sheets, but they all heard it.

Neither Nurse Ratchet nor Caleb's dad had noticed. The phone fight had ended with Nurse Ratchet on the phone and Mr Burroughs darting over to Caleb's bed.

'I've got to go now, son. But I'll be back tomorrow. Don't worry, I'll make sure this shambles gets reported in all the papers and I'll be talking to hospital management. They can't be incompetent when it comes to my son.'

With a short nod to Caleb, Mr Burroughs raced for the door.

Caleb didn't say anything, but he pulled down his sheet to watch his dad leave. His eyes were definitely red.

'We'll keep looking for Barry,' Piotr said firmly.

Caleb looked Piotr right in the eye. He must have seen something there that he liked because he gave a short cough and then said, 'No one's come in to look for Barry. Have you noticed? It's because he lives in the dogs' home. He hasn't got an owner. I think I might be his best friend.

He went missing when he was with me.' His voice faded out and he clutched the sheet tighter.

'We'll find him,' Piotr said. 'We won't give up.'

Just then the ward door buzzed, and Flora and Andrew appeared. Had they found Dr Malcolm? Did they think he was guilty? They weren't smiling the way they might if they had found Barry.

Sylvie climbed on to her bed and stared up at the ceiling. This investigation was in desperate need of a breakthrough.

She listened as Flora and Andrew described their encounter with Dr Malcolm.

'We couldn't see his hands,' Andrew said. 'He wore gloves.'

'Suspicious!' Piotr said.

'Yes. But he also said he was with a slimming club when Barry went missing. So loads of people can give him an alibi.'

Flora noted that down in her book.

'We found another suspect,' Minnie said. 'Nurse Ratchet was on his own in the office when Barry went missing. But he doesn't have a cut on his hands.'

'What do we do next?' Minnie asked.

'We might try to find the Whiter. Or more tall men,'

Andrew replied. 'But, to be honest, I don't know if I can do anything more today. Mum will be wondering where I am.'

'You're not giving up!' Sylvie said hotly.

'Of course not,' Andrew said. 'Piotr made a promise to Caleb and we'll be keeping it. It's just ... well ... I don't know how we can.'

# Chapter Ten

Sylvie spent the rest of the day trying to prove to all the adults that she was responsible. She asked loudly for her insulin before her evening meal. Nurse Adams fetched it from the fridge, and Sylvie was careful to show that she waited until it reached room temperature before injecting it, placing it on her bed table and watching it intently for twenty minutes. She did a blood test before eating, recording the number in her book, waving her pencil like a baton before writing. She did another before bed. She was the perfect diabetes patient – and she made sure that Nurse Adams noticed.

Caleb noticed too. He hardly spoke, but she could feel his eyes following her. And, though she liked being on stage with people watching, she didn't like grouchy boys doing it.

'What?' she said finally, glaring at Caleb.

He shrugged. 'There's not much entertainment around here, and you're putting on a show.'

Sylvie tugged the curtain around her bed closed and flopped on to the mattress. She was not putting on a show, she was being responsible – and doing a good job of it, so far.

The overhead lights were switched off at eight. Older kids were allowed to keep their bedside lights on, but the little kids were expected to go to sleep. The soft voices of patients whispering goodnight to each other, or to their parents on the phone, sounded like waves on the sea. Sylvie felt herself relax. Her eyes drifted closed. She was asleep.

Until a wail woke her.

A small kid crying. The ward was almost dark. Proper night-time. And someone was gasping through sobs.

Sylvie peeped out through her curtain. Across the way, Celine was sitting up in her bed. Her face was twisted and wet globs of tears glistened in the moonlight. Sylvie wondered whether she should get up to comfort her, but before she could move, a night nurse clip-clopped across the floor and had her arms around the little girl.

Sylvie could hear what Celine said through her gasps. 'The Whiter. *Un cauchemar.*'

'A nightmare?' the nurse asked softly. 'Hush, hush, it's all right, you don't need to be scared.'

Sylvie lay back down. The little girl was so frightened by what she'd seen, she was having bad dreams. Who was the Whiter? What was it? Was it a thing or a person?

In the dark, Sylvie stared upwards, sleepless now.

What did the Whiter have to do with the fake maintenance man?

She could hear Celine's sobs quieting to whimpers. She knew how the little girl felt. It was scary to be in the hospital, away from home, with strangers sleeping right beside you. Adults you didn't know telling you what to do. And the worry about being ill.

That was the worst bit, really. She kicked at the sheets that felt too hot. Being ill. The first time she'd stayed at the hospital, the nights had been awful. Lying there, alone, knowing she was never going to be cured – that she was always going to have to live with it. She was always going to be the weird one at school, with mood swings and fainting and watching food and stabbing herself over and over every day. It had been awful. A nightmare.

It had only been the friendly security guard who had made her first night OK. Davey, his name was. He'd patrolled the ward and seen her, lying awake. He hadn't stayed long, just long enough to tell her his name and say he was watching out for them, that she was safe.

She'd felt safe too, just for a little while. His smile had made her feel it might all be all right. She'd slept. That's what Celine needed now – a visit from a security guard to tell her she was safe.

As her eyes began to close again, her brain suddenly fizzed. Davey! The security team would be looking for Barry. They might even have CCTV. They might even have filmed the Whiter!

Sylvie knew she was going to have a hard time sleeping now – she had a new lead and couldn't wait for morning to come.

# Chapter Eleven

Sylvie must have slept, because the sounds of morning on the ward woke her – squeals and barefoot steps, water rushing through pipework, the odd homesick sniffle. She stretched, then remembered Davey and threw back the sheets. She had to get Flora here as soon as possible. And the others. She texted her sister, then went to get her vial of insulin from the nurses' station.

It was Nurse Ratchet there this morning, looking cross. 'We're short-staffed today,' he said.

'Nurse Adams hasn't disappeared, has she? Like Barry?'

Nurse Ratchet scoffed. 'No, she's just running late. Here.' He handed over the bottle from the locked fridge.

'I'll wait for it to warm,' Sylvie said in her most pious, butter-wouldn't-melt voice. But Nurse Ratchet wasn't even listening; there was some crisis with a lost teddy and a single sock that he was forced to get involved with.

Sylvie put the vial on her bedside cabinet and got dressed. She was pulling on her socks when her curtain twitched.

'Knock, knock!' Andrew's voice said. He stepped into her cubicle with Piotr and Flora and Minnie right behind.

'You were quick!' Sylvie said.

'We were on our way anyway,' Flora replied. 'What was so urgent you needed to text? Has something happened?'

'Did you see the Whiter in the night? Wooooo!' Andrew draped the end of the curtain over his head and made ghost hands at them.

'No, but I did think of something,' Sylvie said. She explained about Davey.

'You've got a friend in Security, and you're only just mentioning it now?' Minnie asked.

Sylvie felt her cheeks redden. He wasn't really a friend, just someone who'd been friendly once. She hardly knew him, it was a wonder she'd even remembered his name.

But she really should have thought of him sooner.

'I've remembered now, OK?'

'Shall we go and see if we can find him?' Piotr asked.

Sylvie pushed her feet into her shoes and headed over to Nurse Ratchet, who was crawling on the floor near someone's bed.

'I'm going out for a bit. I won't leave the hospital. I'll be back later. OK?'

'Ha!' He grabbed at a tiny, rolled-up sock. 'Here it is. Oh, Sylvie. Fine. If you must.'

'Do you know where Davey would be?' Flora asked, once they were safely off the ward.

'Security have their office in the basement.'

They climbed down the staircase, down past the atrium that formed the main entrance, and down another floor. The big painted sign read '-1'.

The air was strangely warm and humid. It smelled of soap and the scorched steam of ironing.

'This isn't Security,' Minnie said doubtfully, 'it's more like Laundry.'

'It's this way,' Sylvie said, more confidently than she felt. She set off down the main corridor. It was wide, like the ones on the floors above, but the only light came from harsh strips of halogens above their heads. The sound of lifts whirring and machines clunking came from somewhere close by. Sylvie felt the tendrils of her hair begin to stick to her face in the clammy air.

They came to a T-junction in the corridor; in front of them was a wall of pale bricks. To the left was a row of

84

metal cages, stuffed full of sheets and pillowcases and towels. The laundry. But to their right was a door with the word 'Security' stuck to it, peeling up in the dampness.

Bingo.

There was a glass window set in the centre of the door, criss-crossed with thin wire. Sylvie stood on tiptoes to be able to see inside. A man and a woman sat with their backs to her, watching a bank of ten or twelve screens – each showing grainy images of parts of the hospital. Was the man Davey? It was hard to tell from behind.

Beside her, Andrew danced nervously from foot to foot. Piotr, Minnie and Flora stood their ground, ready to take on anyone. Sylvie raised her fist and rapped smartly on the door.

It opened and the woman peered out. 'Hello,' she said. Her face was hidden underneath a mass of wiry curls, like a squirrel peeping out from a bush. Sylvie tried to peer under her arm.

'Davey?' Sylvie called.

'Hey, what are you doing?' the woman said. 'Don't I know you?'

Sylvie felt herself blush a little. 'Well, I do act. You might have seen me as the cup bearer in *Road to Moscow*, or the housemaid in *The Apple Trees*?'

The woman shook her head. 'No. That's not it. I know –' she clicked her fingers '– you were on the CCTV this morning. Children's ward?'

Minnie barked a laugh. Sylvie didn't deign to respond.

Ignoring the woman, Sylvie ducked down to see into the security office. 'Davey?' she said again.

Inside, the chair turned. It was Davey!

'It's Sylvie, isn't it?' he said, with a soft smile. 'What are you doing down in the depths of this place?'

'We're looking for the lost dog,' she said.

Davey stood and stepped closer, blocking her view of the screens. 'What do you know about the dog?' he asked.

Sylvie rested her hand on the door frame, willing Davey to invite them in, to listen to them.

But Davey stepped in front of the woman and pulled the door close to his body. 'Sylvie, this area is restricted. It isn't meant for chil– for patients,' he said softly. 'Whatever you guys are doing, it's probably best for you to go back to the ward. I can't help.'

'It's not you who can help us, it's us who can help you,' Minnie said firmly. 'Invite us in.'

# Chapter Twelve

Davey stood still in the doorway for a moment. But there was something in Minnie's tone of voice that made him step backwards, opening the door as he did so.

'Davey!' the woman said. 'This is a secure area, you know that. They can't come in.'

'Let's hear them out, Claire,' he said, 'just for five minutes. What harm can it do?' Claire looked at the screens, but shrugged and stepped back to let them in.

The room was small, and it was a tight squeeze to fit all seven of them. As well as the screens, there was a black, shiny desk. It looked like Darth Vader ironed flat. Davey had rested a dirty-looking mug of tea a bit too close to the computer keyboard. There were two chairs and a noticeboard with A4 printouts of camera images – timestamped people crossing the tiled floors and corridors of the hospital above them.

'You better explain what this is all about,' Davey said with a sigh.

'We are investigators with lots of experience,' Minnie said, 'and we think we can help you find Barry.'

'Assuming you are actually looking for Barry,' Sylvie said, looking directly at Claire.

'The missing dog?' Claire replied. 'We've run sweeps of the building. Every door in non-public areas can only be opened with passes. There's no unusual pass activity. We've checked the CCTV. There's no sign of him. He's probably just gone home.'

Sylvie looked at the screens. People flitted across them, jerky and pixelated with the time delay. Was there really no sign of Caleb's dog?

'There must have been something on the cameras,' Flora said desperately.

'Nothing unusual,' Davey said. 'We've printed out the images and gone through them. No strangers on the ward. No sign of the dog.' He rested his hand on a small stack of papers beside his mug.

'Can we take a look?' Minnie asked.

Davey shook his head. 'Data protection. We can't let just anyone look through CCTV images.'

Sylvie opened her mouth, ready to argue, when the door flew open.

A woman, in the same dark uniform as Davey and Claire, stood filling the doorway. Her arms and legs were spread in an X, her whole body rigid with tension. Her dark hair was scraped taut, like a frightened cat perched on her head.

Davey leaped to his feet. Even Claire smartened up, holding her head high, her eyes facing forward.

'What exactly,' the new arrival said, 'are these children doing in what is meant to be a restricted area? Have they been recruited to the security team? I certainly don't remember interviewing them for the job.' Her sarcasm seemed to cut through Davey like a hot knife through butter. He wilted under her gaze.

'No, ma'am. Sorry, ma'am. They were just … visiting,' he finished lamely.

'Well, visiting hours are over!' the woman said sternly. 'You two, we've got a situation!'

The two security staff stepped forward, ready for action. 'What is it, ma'am?'

'This dog incident has reached a new level. One Mr Burroughs, apparently a relative of a patient, has alerted the press.'

Sylvie kept one ear on the conversation, but edged –
softly, slowly – towards the desk.

'Reporters have been calling. The switchboard has lit
up like a Christmas tree. Everyone wants to know what
we're doing about it.'

'It's just a dog,' Claire said.

The freezing stare that Ma'am gave Claire was fierce
enough to start a new ice age. 'A dog who went missing
from a children's ward. And if we can lose a dog, the
reporters are saying, we can lose a child. This is a disaster.'

Sylvie was at the desk now, her back to the dirty mug.
Her fingers on the sheaf of papers.

'Everyone needs to drop whatever they are doing,'
Ma'am said, 'and find that dog, pronto! Which means
no more chatting to civilians. You lot, out!' She pointed a
jabby finger at the gang. 'Now!'

Andrew shuffled out first. The others followed, Sylvie
keeping her back to Ma'am the whole time.

'Good luck finding Barry,' she said.

Ma'am stomped into the security room, and Sylvie
could hear her yelling instructions. All the team was to be
pulled in for a briefing, from every part of the hospital,
that instant.

Sylvie ducked into an alcove set in the mouldering

90

brickwork of the basement. It was designed to help support the curved ceiling, but it was also a discreet spot to show the others what she was holding.

Piotr gasped. 'The CCTV images! You've taken them.'

'Borrowed them,' Sylvie said. 'I'll put them back in a minute. Do you want to look at them or not?'

Sylvie held five or six pieces of paper. The top one showed Nurse Ratchet standing outside the children's ward with his head in his hands. The others below were still a mystery.

Flora was frowning at her. 'We shouldn't be looking at them. Davey said so.'

Sylvie felt a prickle of guilt turning her cheeks red. She'd seen an opportunity and taken it. Surely Flora would see that? 'I'll take them straight back, if you want?' Sylvie offered.

She turned to go back.

But Minnie grabbed her arm. 'It can't hurt to take a quick look,' she said.

With a grin, Sylvie handed a piece of paper to everyone.

'Nurse Ratchet,' Andrew said.

'Me too. He takes lots of breaks,' Piotr added.

'I've got Mum and Sylvie!' Flora said with a smile.

'They won't mind me looking at their picture.' There was relief in her voice.

'I've got Nurse Adams arriving with the three dogs,' Sylvie said.

They all looked at Minnie. She turned her page so that they could all see it. 'A man with a laundry cart,' she said.

'A tall, dark-haired man with a laundry cart,' Piotr said.

Was it the man she'd seen on the stairwell? Sylvie peered at the grainy snapshot. It was hard to tell. It could easily be, though.

Flora gasped. 'Celine is from France, right?'

Sylvie nodded.

'*Blanchisseur!*' Flora said.

'Bless you,' Andrew replied.

'No! *Blanchisseur* is the French for laundryman! I remember from last time we were on holiday and Dad got chocolate on his shirt. And *blanchisserie* is French for laundrette.'

Sylvie nodded.

'And if you were a little French girl trying to translate *blanchisseur* into English …'

Sylvie caught on instantly – she knew her French colours, at least. 'You'd call him the Whiter!' she said. '*Blanc* is French for white!'

'The laundrette stole Barry?' Andrew asked.

'Or the laundryman stole Barry. Celine was trying to tell us all along.'

Piotr slapped the brickwork in delight. 'Security staff wouldn't be suspicious of a laundryman. He must do his rounds all the time. And he'd have access to the uniforms too. He could get his hands on a maintenance overall really easily.'

'Does he have a cut on his hand?' Flora asked.

Minnie peered closely at the photo. She angled it into the light. 'He's got a plaster on his finger,' she said finally.

At last. They'd found their suspect.

# Chapter Thirteen

'Come on,' Flora said, 'we need to get to the laundry.'

They turned towards the humid scent of soap. The hospital laundry was in the basement too. But they found themselves looking at a pack of security staff. The uniformed guards spilled out of the office into the corridor like a flock of black sheep waiting to be barked at.

And they were being barked at. Ma'am's voice snapped out demands and commands. Get leads, get sightings, get intel. The people in the corridor continued looking sheepish – they had no idea what to do first.

Sylvie knew what to do. She snatched the image from Minnie's hands. 'Hey!' Minnie protested. But Sylvie ignored her. She stomped back along the corridor and ploughed into the crowd. The dark uniforms were pressed tightly together, smelling of sweat and perfume and soap.

She elbowed her way through, forcing a passage between hips and elbows until she was back in the office.

The press of bodies was even tighter in here. Every security guard in the hospital must have been crammed into the small space. Ma'am was right at the centre of the crowd, yelling.

'Our jobs are at stake here! We find the dog, or we're all out on our ears. Management have made that quite clear.'

She was shouting so hard wisps of hair had come loose from her ponytail, fanning out like a mane around her head. 'We need to keep this hospital out of the newspapers. So find me someone to go after!'

'Here!' Sylvie stood on tiptoes and waved the sheet of paper like a white flag. The bodies moved ever so slightly around her, giving her enough space to wriggle to the front. 'Here!' she said again. 'Here's your suspect. He came into the children's ward with a laundry trolley. One of the children saw him take the dog. He was also seen tampering with computer files earlier in the day. We believe he is a hospital employee.'

Ma'am gave herself a small shake, like a dog getting dry. 'Didn't I just tell you to leave?' she asked Sylvie.

'I came back,' Sylvie said. 'With the lead you were looking for.'

Ma'am pressed her lips firmly closed. Sylvie flapped the piece of paper again. Would Ma'am take it? Would she listen to them? She had to!

Then Ma'am gave a tight nod and snatched the sheet from Sylvie's hand. She stared at it for a second or two. Then she held it above her head. 'All units to the laundry immediately. Find me this man – and the dog!'

There was a sudden stampede. Sylvie swayed and almost fell as all the black-clad bodies around her emptied into the corridor, then sprinted to the right – heading for the laundry. Ma'am was right behind them. In seconds, Sylvie was alone in the security office.

Flora stuck her head around the door. 'What did you do?' she asked.

'Sent them to the laundry!'

'Well, come on, hurry, let's get after them!'

It was easy to find the laundry – even without the ranks of security staff who swarmed down stairwells and spilled into corridors – they just had to follow the heat. It was like running into a hot cloud. Soon, the white tiled walls were obscured by trolleys of linen bags stuffed with dirty sheets and towels, and rows of aluminium shelves neatly stacked with clean blue-and-white pillowcases and gowns. Wisps of steam twisted in the air like damp candyfloss.

Sylvie could see Davey and Claire every now and again. They ran at the head of the line. Heavy boots clattered and clumped along the corridor. From somewhere nearby they heard a dog bark.

Barry?

Sylvie tried to pick up the pace, but her legs felt heavy.

Ma'am called orders at the guards. 'Get these doors open! Fan out, check every corner, call the dog's name. Let's do this! Find the dog, find the thief!'

In seconds the guards had spread out. The main corridor had anterooms and storage spaces opening off it, all closed with heavy security doors. Black-clad figures held white security passes against readers, turning the access lights from red to green. All along the corridor, doors opened and the guards dipped into each room. But most of the noise and steam came from a big room at the end of the corridor. It was as though a dragon was snoring inside. It was there that most of the guards headed, with Piotr, Minnie, Andrew, Flora and Sylvie right behind. Ma'am held up her pass and the door clicked open.

Inside, a wall of huge washing machines, big enough to take duvets and blankets, ran down one side. Most of them were switched on and suds and sheets whirled inside. Bang, whack, slam, smack – super-sized spin cycles thumped and walloped. All around, guards in black uniforms swiped sweat from brows before bending to look under tables and ironing boards and racks of clean uniforms.

There was one other person in the room. A woman. She wore maroon overalls and clutched a box of washing powder like a security blanket. She watched the army of guards in confusion.

Ma'am stopped in front of her. 'Wher' za 'og?' she yelled.

The woman cupped her hand to her ear. 'Wha'?'

'Za 'og? Wher' ze?'

The woman shrugged.

Ma'am's face turned red with heat and frustration. She stalked over to the washing machines and slammed her fist on to the power buttons, one at a time. In moments the whirling machines had calmed to a gentle rocking, then they were quiet.

'Hey!' the woman said. 'You can't turn those off.'

'I can, and I have,' Ma'am replied. 'There's a dog here somewhere. Where is it?'

'Show her the picture,' Sylvie called.

Ma'am looked annoyed to see that the gang were still with her units, but she handed the CCTV printout to the woman. 'We're looking for this man. We believe he has a missing dog.'

The woman cradled her washing powder under her arm and took the sheet with her free hand. She gave it the shortest glance in the world. 'John?' she snapped. 'You're looking for John? He was in this morning.'

'Where is he now?'

'I don't know. He never tells me anything. I haven't seen him for about half an hour. He's been distracted all day, watching the corridors like they were going to explode. Him and that dog. Dogs aren't allowed, of course. Not that John cares, he does what he likes.'

'The dog was here? Where is it now?'

Another shrug.

Ma'am was on her radio at once. 'Suspect has left the laundry. I repeat, suspect is on the move. Check exits, get me a sighting!'

The effect was instant. The guards swirled through the door like water down a plughole. Moments later, Ma'am's radio crackled: 'Ma'am, come in. There's a white van in the car park. I think there's a dog in the passenger seat. I'm in pursuit.'

'I'm on my way!' Ma'am cried. She holstered her radio and bolted for the door.

'I'm on my way too!' Andrew yelled.

'Go! Go!' Sylvie said. 'I'm not supposed to leave the hospital.'

Andrew, Minnie and Piotr tore after the disappearing guards. They pelted through an emergency door at the end of the corridor, then up a short flight of stairs and found themselves, in a burst of sudden sunlight, surrounded by sea-grey tarmac. The car park.

'There!' Davey yelled.

In the distance, a white van was racing between warehouses. A guard raced after it, but was falling behind. The van screeched to the right, then was gone from view.

'We've lost him,' Davey said. He slumped on to a concrete bollard and dropped his head into his hands.

Piotr felt his heart twist for Davey. He patted the man awkwardly on the shoulder. He'd seen Dad do it with his own friends. For Dad it seemed to say everything he wanted, without him having to explain what he was feeling.

Piotr wasn't sure he'd got it entirely right, but Davey seemed to appreciate the thought. 'You're a good lad,' he said gruffly.

'He is!' Andrew agreed. 'But an even better detective. This isn't the end of this case.'

Davey looked sceptical.

'Seriously! He's one of the best under-sixteen detectives in the whole town.'

'Are there many competitors for that title?' Davey asked.

'You'd be surprised,' Andrew said.

Ma'am stalked up to their knot of people. 'Did any of you see the driver? Or the number plate?'

Everyone shook their heads.

'What about Barry? Did you get a look at him?'

More shakes.

'Really?' Ma'am turned slowly, taking in every member of her team, like the harsh beam of a lighthouse. 'Every single guard in this hospital is out here. We have the best security system, and none of you saw anything useful?'

Silence.

'Well, that's brilliant,' she said. She kicked the lowest rung of the fire escape with her steel-toe-capped boot. It clanged like a broken bell. 'Just brilliant.'

# Chapter Fourteen

Sylvie and Flora stood in the middle of the big laundry room, alone with the woman.

'I'm Flora, this is Sylvie,' Flora said hopefully.

'Tania,' the woman said, 'I'm supposed to be in charge of the laundry, but that idiot of a guard has just ruined that spin cycle.' She looked at the silent machines in disgust. 'Who does she think she is?'

She pulled open the door of the nearest machine. The seal gave with a wet squelch and drips of water splatted on to the lino floor. 'Still sopping! I'll have to start all over again. That's an hour wasted. And they'll blame me when there's no clean sheets.'

Sylvie looked at the well-stocked racks that lined one wall. There were hundreds of sheets there. But she was getting a strong sense that Tania wasn't someone who would see reason easily.

'Can we help at all?' Flora asked.

What? Sylvie didn't know the first thing about washing machines, or ironing! When she was older she was only ever going to wear Lycra and wool – things that stayed flat of their own accord. She threw Flora a look which clearly said, 'You're ironing alone.'

But Tania gave a mirthless laugh. 'No, I'm used to doing this all by myself.'

'Doesn't John work here too?' Flora asked.

Tania scooped washing powder and dumped it in a dispensing drawer. She rammed the drawer closed. 'If by work you mean sit drinking tea and reading magazines all day, then, yes, John works here. If you mean getting any of the laundry done, then, no, I'm on my tod down here.' She jabbed a few buttons and the machines began to turn slowly.

'What do you know about John?'

Tania tutted. 'I don't know. No one ever tells me any thing. They think that all their clean uniforms come from the laundry fairy. They forget about us down here. You know three of my machines are broken? I complain and what happens? Nothing.' The machines picked up pace, almost in time with Tania's grumbles. Thump – moan – thump – moan.

Sylvie wasn't all that surprised that John didn't talk to Tania much.

'Do you know his full name?'

'John Doe,' Tania said.

'Really?' Flora sounded doubtful.

'Yes, really. Why would I lie?' Tania snapped.

'Sorry,' Flora said. 'Is there anything else you can tell us?'

'I can tell you plenty. That management couldn't care less about what goes on down here. That they'll take for ever to replace John, assuming he isn't coming back. If he did steal that dog, I suppose he won't.'

'But about John,' Flora pressed. 'What do you know about him?'

'He's a waste of space. Pass me that basket, would you? Hey, you two look really similar, did you know that?'

They were getting nothing from Tania.

Back in the main corridor, Andrew, Minnie and Piotr trudged behind the security team. The guards were like wilting tulips, with their heads down and nothing to say. They had been so close to getting Barry back. He'd only been a short walk from the security office the whole time!

Sylvie and Flora met the others as they trooped past.

'Nothing?' Sylvie asked, reading the expression of gloomy misery on everyone's faces.

'We missed him,' Piotr said simply.

'The laundry lady, Tania, told us that John was lazy and read magazines all the time. But I get the feeling she likes to complain, so who knows if it's true.'

'And,' Flora said seriously, 'I don't think John is even his real name. Tania told us that John's full name is John Doe. That's the name the police use when they have an unidentified victim. I think he must have picked that name as a joke.'

'How can we find someone who's using a fake name?' Andrew asked.

They headed away from the steamy, damp walls of the laundry, back towards the climate-controlled comfort of the public area. Sylvie dragged her feet as she climbed the stairs. Her head still felt stuffed full of humid air, as though it had seeped into her skull and wrapped her thoughts in heavy blankets.

'Maybe we can go back to Heather and ask to see his employment file?' Sylvie suggested. Her tongue felt strangely thick in her mouth. 'His address would be on his record.'

Flora stopped, stunned.

Sylvie headbutted her back. 'Ow!'

'He won't have an employment file! Of course! That's what he was doing in her office! Wiping his own file. He knew he was going to steal Barry yesterday, so he wiped his own records so that they can't trace him.'

Sylvie wished she could sit down. She felt so tired all of a sudden. 'I was about to say that,' she snapped.

'Well, you weren't quick enough,' Minnie replied.

It was no use. She had to sit. Sylvie dropped on to the stair and leaned heavily against the wall.

'Are you OK?' Piotr asked. His voice seemed to come to her from a long way away, as though he were back in the laundry and she was hearing the echo as he spoke. The edges of her vision darkened. In the pinhole that was left, she saw Flora's face.

She felt herself being lifted. Hands around her arms and legs and shoulders. Up in the air. Weightless. Movement. Sound. Colour. And none of it made any sense at all.

# Chapter Fifteen

Sylvie could hear Flora's voice. It had the same end-of-the-corridor-ness that Piotr's voice had had. When was that? Yesterday? Today?

'Drink this.' Flora's voice again.

She felt narrow plastic on her lips. Smelled sweetness.

'Please, drink.'

Sylvie sucked the straw. Tasted sugar. And orange. She felt her own heartbeat in her ears, quick and erratic. Another sip. Another. She felt Flora's hand on her arm. What had happened? As the sugary drink took effect, she realised. A hypo. Her blood sugar had dropped dangerously low.

The hypo had come from nowhere!

No. That wasn't true.

Her insulin vial was still sitting, warming, on her bedside table.

She'd done no blood test, had no breakfast.

She felt her eyes sting with tears. How could she have been so stupid? She'd been so sure she'd be able to care for herself. She'd been so wrapped up in the mystery, so excited by having a lead, that she'd forgotten to pay any attention to herself. Dr Malcolm was going to say she'd failed. And Mum would say she'd told Sylvie so. And Mum would be choosing her meals and nagging her about tests until she was thirty.

'Is she OK? I mean, Sylvie, are you OK?' Piotr asked.

She would be. It usually didn't take long for the sugar to reach her bloodstream. But the crossness would take longer to fade. Crossness with herself.

'I'm an idiot.' Sylvie closed her eyes, waited for Minnie to agree.

But Minnie said nothing.

Was she so disgusted with Sylvie that she couldn't even speak?

She opened her eyes. Minnie was sitting across the table. Her mouth was soft with concern. Her brown eyes glistened like fresh conkers. Were those tears? Sylvie couldn't speak. There was a lump in her own throat that sips of fizzy orange couldn't shift. She stared at the table instead; its ugly shade of beige was safe. Soothing.

Flora unzipped her backpack and took out a small white packet. 'You didn't even have any glucose tablets in your pocket. I checked. Take these. Do you want to go and see Dr Malcolm?'

'No!' Sylvie took the packet sheepishly. She had been a total idiot. 'Please don't tell him this happened? Please?' she begged.

She spotted the looks that flashed between the others. They wanted to tell him.

'No! Please. This won't happen again. I'll be more careful.' Her hands tightened around the drink can; she could feel the metal buckling.

'We can't lie,' Piotr said. 'It's too important. But we can say that we won't let anyone know unless they ask us directly. Is that fair?'

Sylvie nodded miserably. Mum was bound to ask Flora, or Dr Malcolm would. It was bound to come out. They'd lost Barry. They'd lost their lead. And she was probably going to lose her one shot at being in charge of her own life.

The day couldn't get much worse.

She dropped her head into her hands and let the

coolness of the table drain the heat from her cheeks. With her eyes closed, the cafe chatter began to sound like water again, soothing babble running over mossy rocks.

Flora rubbed her back gently. 'Don't worry. We can go back to the ward and you can do a blood test. And you'll be back on track again. It isn't the end of the world.'

Sylvie hated that phrase. People said it to her a lot.

She shrugged off Flora's hand and lifted her head.

She needed a minute by herself.

There was that bench, she remembered, in front of Dame Julie Dent's picture. She sat there sometimes. She stood up. 'I'll go back to the ward. In a minute.'

She turned to where the painting hung.

And saw an empty wall.

What? She stepped towards it, slowly, carefully.

'What is it?' Flora asked. 'Where are you going?'

Sylvie didn't reply.

'Sylvie!'

The air felt thick; she had to concentrate to keep moving. She was still feeling the effects of the hypo. The reception desk. They would know where the picture had gone. Her legs felt rubbery, her pulse quick again. Flora was right by her side. When she reached the desk, she rested both her palms on the surface, pressing down to keep herself upright. She heard footsteps as the others came to join them.

'Where's the painting?' Sylvie said. She pointed to the bare space on the pale wall. There was a lighter rectangle still visible, with a dusty tide marking its edges.

The woman who was sitting behind the desk followed Sylvie's finger.

'Oh. A guard had to move it. It's gone into storage.'

'A guard?'

'Yes, someone from security. He had a badge and a clipboard.'

A dark feeling grew inside Sylvie. A kind of dread. 'When?'

'Oh, maybe fifteen or twenty minutes ago.'

'No.'

The woman nervously tapped her immaculate black hair into place. 'What do you mean?'

Andrew leaped up and leaned over the desk. His arms wedged him in place while his feet dangled above the tiles. 'What she means is, fifteen or twenty minutes ago every single security guard in this hospital was chasing a man and a dog. None of them had time to move a painting. So, who did?'

Behind the desk, the woman's face turned pale beneath

her layer of make-up. Her eyes flicked to the wall, to Andrew, to the wall.

'Was it worth a lot of money?' Andrew asked.

'It was a Minet,' the woman whispered. 'On loan to the hospital. Worth about three million pounds.'

'Oops,' Andrew said.

# Chapter Sixteen

The receptionist's hand was shaking as she reached for the phone. 'He was so convincing,' she said. 'He must have been a real guard. He must have been.' She dialled, getting the number wrong twice, before the call connected. 'Security? This is Shazia at the front desk. Did one of your team just take the Minet?'

Sylvie watched her face carefully. Whatever the person at the other end of the line was saying, it drained all colour from Shazia's cheeks. Bad news.

Shazia hung up. She stared at the phone as though she was waiting for it to wake her from a bad dream.

'It was just on loan. I'm going to be in so much trouble. The hospital management will be furious. Dame Julie, who owns it, will be broken-hearted. Even the government will be angry! They give her a tax refund for sharing the art. It's a charity scheme that's never gone wrong before. What if the prime minister hears?'

'Deep breaths,' Minnie advised.

Shazia's eyes flicked upwards, to look at Minnie. 'It must just be a mistake? A misunderstanding? There's usually a security guard nearby all the time.' Her lower lip wobbled. Then she burst into tears.

There was a box of tissues next to a potted orchid on the reception desk. Tears must be quite common, Sylvie thought as she plucked a few tissues from the box. Shazia took them and blew noisily.

'I'm going to lose my job.'

'No, it was an honest mistake,' Piotr said. 'It's hard to argue with someone who has a clipboard.'

'And a badge,' Andrew added.

Shazia wailed and covered her face with the tissues.

Then Sylvie heard pounding footsteps – Ma'am and Davey running across Reception. Ma'am was out of breath when she slammed her palm down on the desk. 'Shazia. Everything you know. Now.'

More security staff were following behind. Sylvie saw them move to stand by the entrance, by the stairwell, beneath the space where the painting had been, silently standing guard. A bit late for that.

'I was sitting here,' Shazia said, 'when a man – tall, wearing a security uniform – came in. He said the painting had been recalled and he had to put it in storage. He showed me his clipboard. He had an order on hospital paper. He looked so genuine. And he had one of those yellow signs that says "Caution". He put out the sign, climbed some little mini steps, and took down the painting. Then carried the whole lot out. I didn't think anything of it. I'm so stupid.'

Ma'am made a kind of coughing noise that indicated that she totally agreed.

Flora spoke up. 'Maybe it really was a security guard? Maybe they were telling the truth?'

'Do you think so?' Shazia looked up hopefully.

'No!' Ma'am snapped. 'I do not think so. I know what every member of my team is doing at any moment. And if any of them had been told to move a valuable painting, they would tell me. *I* run a tight ship.' She drew out the 'I', making it clear that she thought the rest of the hospital ran a very loose ship indeed – especially Reception.

'Barry was a decoy dog,' Piotr said softly.

Around the reception desk, everyone turned to look at Piotr. His eyes flashed with understanding. 'Barry was used to distract everyone. Especially the security guards. Normally there's a guard by the painting, yes?'

'And another one on the main entrance, just there,' Sylvie added, pointing to the door only metres from the reception desk.

'Well,' Piotr continued, 'to steal the painting, John needed to get all the guards out of the way for a while. What better way to do that than to cause panic on the children's ward? It worked perfectly.'

Ma'am's face went from stern statue to jittery jelly. 'You mean he tricked us?'

'Exactly. He made sure that all of the guards in the hospital were on a wild goose chase in the basement, while the real crime happened right here in broad daylight. He must have been waiting for the moment when all the guards were called away.'

Ma'am pulled herself together and up to her full height. Which was not very tall. But the look on her face was enough to make anyone do what she said. It was the sort of look an eagle might give a rabbit before swooping it into the air. 'Right. No one leaves this area until they have been interviewed. We need to get the police here, with scene-of-crime officers right behind them. This has been a very bad day for this hospital, but we are going to put it right.'

'Yeah!' Andrew said, pumping his fist into the air.

'Not you,' Ma'am said. 'I have no idea why you've

been there every time I've turned around today. Perhaps I should treat you lot with suspicion?'

Minnie bristled like an angry cat. 'We have been helping! Who told you about the Whiter? About John in the first place?'

Ma'am turned her eagle look on Minnie. 'Right now, I don't know what to think. Which means you lot have to go and sit quietly at one of those tables and wait until you can be properly interviewed. You do not move out of my sight. Understood?'

The others turned, ready to head back to the table, but Sylvie stayed put. She planted her hands on her hips defiantly. 'Actually,' she said, 'I have to go back to the children's ward. I need to do a blood test.'

Ma'am frowned.

'It's a medical emergency,' Sylvie added.

'Fine! But I want you back down here as soon as possible for a full debrief,' Ma'am said.

They took it slowly as they walked back to the ward. Sylvie kept her hand on the banister, still feeling a little wonky. But they all talked as they climbed. Barry had only been stolen to distract the guards! The real target was Dame Julie's painting. There was a much bigger conspiracy at work!

Nurse Ratchet let them in with a scowl. He seemed to need three pairs of arms today to deal with all the jobs he was trying to do. Hopefully he hadn't noticed the unused insulin by her bed.

Sylvie did a quick blood test and ate an energy bar from the bag Mum had packed for her. She was feeling better every second.

Minnie was standing beside Caleb's bed. He looked very pale, almost transparent. His eyes were partly closed. 'We think Barry was taken by art thieves,' Minnie told him.

His eyes snapped open. 'What?'

Minnie explained as best she could. She told him about the hunt through the laundry, and the van, and the fake guard with a clipboard.

Caleb shook his head gently. 'Poor Barry. They'd better look after him properly or they'll have my dad to answer to.'

Caleb was right, his dad was pretty fierce. Something occurred to Sylvie. 'How did your dad know Barry was missing? Did you tell him?'

Caleb shook his head. 'No. He got a call from someone, I think.'

'John?' Piotr asked.

Caleb shrugged. 'Dad runs his own company. He's used to people asking for his help. I don't think he even took the caller's name.'

Sylvie settled on to her bed, running her hand over the sheet, smoothing it flat as she thought. 'John's clever. He knew that telling your dad would mean Ma'am's team would get told off. He has access to all the uniforms in the hospital, but he chose to steal Barry while wearing his own laundry uniform, so that Ma'am would go looking in the laundry, giving him time to commit the real crime.'

'And not just him,' Andrew said. 'Someone was driving the van while John stole the painting. He has an accomplice.'

Two thieves? Two crimes? This was getting complicated.

'We need to tell the police what we know,' Piotr said. 'Let's go and see if we can find Jimmy.'

# Chapter Seventeen

'I'm going to eat lunch at the cafe,' Sylvie told Nurse Ratchet loudly. He mumbled something in her direction, while trying to carry three pillows. 'Then,' she continued, 'the police and the head of security want to interview me. I'm planning on helping them find the missing Minet.'

'Well, just find your way back here before bedtime and we'll all be happy,' Nurse Ratchet said over the top of the bundle.

On their way back down to the cafe, Flora called Jimmy.

Jimmy answered on the second ring. 'Flora, what can I do for you? I can't talk for long, I'm afraid. We're being called out to a major crime at the hospital.'

'Oh, good, you're on your way?'

'I should have known you'd be one step ahead of me,' he laughed. 'You'd better explain.'

So, Flora told him what had happened.

The atrium space was full of people when they got back there, guards, patients and public. While Flora talked to Jimmy, Minnie and Andrew went to get food. Sylvie lolled into a chair and stared at the empty wall where the painting had hung. The stolen scene. Like a great diva storming offstage, the painting's absence was more dramatic than its presence. Hundreds of people walked past it every day and paid no attention. Now it was gone, the whole world was interested. It was an odd phenomenon.

Outside, a van with the logo of a news channel on its side pulled up. Sylvie sat up straight. Cameras! There would be cameras. Should she go and brush her hair?

The journalist who tumbled out of the van was eased back by security. Security were joined in moments by police officers. Then the hospital door slid open to a torrent of officers and scene of crime technicians. Everyone was talking at once. Swiftly, the atrium was filled with the clamour and crush of rapid shouts, instructions, rolls of crime-scene tape, waves of people.

Their own table was an island in the midst of the noise.

'Where's Jimmy?' Minnie asked, arriving with sandwiches to share.

There seemed to be one man in charge. He was directing the flow of people, sending some to the basement, others to interview Shazia, yet more to the children's ward. Soon the bare wall was being dusted for fingerprints, daubs of white powder splattering the surface. All this attention? The painting was definitely a diva.

It was ten minutes, and three shared packets of crisps, before they saw Jimmy. He'd stopped to talk to the man in charge, then he came over.

'Jimmy!' Flora stood and gave him a tight hug. 'I'm so glad you're on the case!'

Jimmy smiled, his blue eyes crinkled with warmth. 'They don't put a lowly constable like me on the theft of a Minet! No, the detectives are the leads on this case. I'm just here for grunt work and crowd control. What are you doing here? Is everyone all right?'

Flora nodded and reassured him that no one was poorly – or at least, not more poorly than normal. 'Sylvie is here on a kind of trial. Not a legal trial, a medical one, for her diabetes. Then Barry went missing and we got all caught up in the mystery.'

Jimmy pulled up a chair and sat down at their table. 'Ah yes, the decoy dog.'

'Yes!' Andrew said. 'They stole Barry but they didn't

even want a dog, they just wanted a distraction. It's not right.'

'Flora, show Jimmy your notebook,' Piotr said.

Flora unzipped her backpack and handed the book to Jimmy. He flipped through, reading her notes. He gave a long whistle. 'You have found out a lot. This is great work. Are you happy for me to show it to the detective inspector in charge?'

'Of course!' Piotr agreed.

Sylvie wished they'd been able to find Barry and maybe even the stolen painting before having to hand over all the evidence. But, she supposed, sometimes you just had to be a team player and dance in the chorus. Being a team player was rubbish.

Jimmy took the notebook and went to talk to the detective inspector.

'I guess we leave it all to the police now,' Andrew said. He laid his head cheek down on the cafe table.

'I wish we didn't have to,' Minnie said. 'Even though it is Jimmy.'

'You know what I wish,' Flora said sadly. 'I wish we'd never got involved in the first place.'

Andrew's head shot up from the table and he stared at Flora in outrage. 'Why?'

'Because we were the ones who led all the guards down to the basement. We made the connection between the CCTV image and the Whiter. We gave them the lead and it led us all into disaster.'

Was it true? Was it their fault that the painting had been stolen? Had they given the thieves their opportunity? All the noise and babble in the atrium seemed to be pressing in on Sylvie's ears. Her skin was tight with the pressure of it. It couldn't be true.

In moments, Jimmy came back. He was smiling. 'DI Morgan is as impressed with you as I am. He thinks you've done great work. He's sending in the teams to find this John character.' He handed the notebook back to Flora.

'How will you find him?' Flora asked.

'We've got ways! Just because you erase a hard drive it doesn't mean the files are gone for good. Our IT guys will go through the database with a fine-tooth comb. They'll find John's record.'

'Will it be enough?' Andrew asked.

Jimmy waved his hand at the scene before them. Police in uniform were taking statements from the customers sitting at the tables. Excited-looking nurses were queueing to share what they knew. Even doctors, usually too busy to notice what was going on outside their office doors, were hanging around, waiting to see what would happen next.

'There must be someone here,' Jimmy said, 'who knows who this man is. We'll get a good statement, or a fingerprint from the laundry, or someone will recognise his picture. We'll get him, don't you worry. The painting will be back on that wall before you can say Jack Sparrow.'

'Jack Sparrow,' Andrew said.

'Well, maybe a bit longer than that,' Jimmy admitted.

# Chapter Eighteen

They had handed all their information over to Jimmy, and answered all the questions they could. They hung around for a while, until it was clear that there was nothing left for them to do but head back to the ward. Sylvie trudged up the staircase. The others walked her as far as the double doors. Then stopped.

'We should let you rest,' Piotr said.

'What?' Sylvie asked.

'We should let you get some sleep, or something.' Piotr's gaze dropped to his feet under the intensity of Sylvie's laser glare.

'Come on, Sylvie,' Piotr mumbled.

'You did nearly faint,' Minnie said.

'I did not,' Sylvie snapped. She might have come close, but she definitely didn't faint. It wasn't even *called* fainting.

'You so did!' Minnie insisted.

Sylvie planted her hands on her hips and put her feet slightly apart. 'I did not nearly faint, I had a hypo. It's totally different.'

Minnie clicked her tongue against her teeth dismissively.

Sylvie felt herself getting angry. 'Well, it is different, and if you'd been paying any attention to me at all, you'd know it too.'

Minnie tilted her head to the side. Her voice was scornful. 'That's your problem, isn't it? No one paying you any attention?'

What? That just wasn't true! Now Sylvie felt her heart thumping hard and fast. 'Are you saying I had a hypo just to get attention?'

'No! I never said that. Did I say that?' Minnie looked at the others for support. Piotr raised his hands. Andrew frowned. And Flora looked as though she wanted the corridor to open up and swallow her.

'Listen,' Piotr said, 'Sylvie, no one meant anything. We just thought you might like to have a bit of peace for a while.'

'You want to get rid of me, don't you?' Even as she said it, she could hear how silly it sounded. Babyish even. But she couldn't stop it. It was as though she was a puppet and her brain wasn't the one controlling her mouth. She had no idea who was.

'Don't be daft,' Minnie said.

'I'm not daft! And I know when I'm not wanted. I don't want to hang around with you anyway. I'd rather be by myself.'

'Fine with me.'

Sylvie made a noise that was half growl, half scream. Then she jabbed her finger hard on to the buzzer. In seconds the door clicked, indicating it had been unlocked. She wrenched it open and stomped into the children's ward without a backwards glance. A diva waltzing away from the scene.

'Sylvie …' she heard Flora say.

But she carried on walking. She heard the door close behind her. Were any of them going to follow her in? Were any of them going to say sorry? She didn't want to turn around to check. There were no footsteps behind her. She forced her head to stay looking forward. They weren't coming.

As she stomped past the nurses' station, she heard Nurse Ratchet call out. 'Sylvie Hampshire, a word, please.'

Sylvie thought about carrying right on past, pretending not to have heard. But there was something about the steely way that Nurse Ratchet spoke that made her slow down. She glanced over. Nurse Ratchet wasn't alone. Dr Malcolm stood beside him, arms folded, frowning.

'What?' Sylvie snapped.

'How's the trial going?' Dr Malcolm asked smoothly.

'Fine!' There was no need to tell him about the hypo, or the forgotten vial, or the fact she'd asked her friends to lie for her. She felt her cheeks redden.

'Really?' Dr Malcolm asked.

'You do know a painting has been stolen, don't you?' Sylvie said, in her best diva onstage voice. 'There are more important things going on than a poxy old blood test.'

'What poxy blood test?' Dr Malcolm raised an eyebrow inquisitively.

Sylvie felt her eyes prickle uncomfortably with tears. This was a horrible day. She wished it had never got started. 'Nothing!' She turned her head sharply and stalked away from the nurses' station.

Behind her back, she could hear Nurse Ratchet saying something to Dr Malcolm about responsibility and proving yourself. But she blocked it out.

The curtain had been pulled back and her bed looked clean and fresh and she thought how nice it would be to curl up under the covers and ignore everyone and everything until she was old enough to be in charge of her own life. She kicked off her shoes, not bothering to tuck them under her bed the way she was supposed to. She climbed under the sheet, in her regular clothes, and pulled it up over her head.

With the white cotton tented over her, and Teddy snuggled under her arm it felt like she was safe from the world. She pressed her fingers against her eyelids until she saw colours and shapes zooming across the blackness. She wasn't going to cry. She wasn't. It was bad enough that she had had a hypo and the others wanted to tell Dr Malcolm. But for them to then push her away as though she was a bad smell just made it worse. She felt wetness against her fingertips. And there was the fact that if she hadn't taken the CCTV image to the security office then the guards wouldn't have been pulled away from the painting. It wouldn't have been stolen. She'd thought she was helping. She'd been so proud of them for working out Celine's clue that she had walked straight into a trap.

The tears were flowing freely now, splashing on to the

mattress. She let herself cry. Today was too awful. And no one cared.

She sniffed.

That wasn't quite true.

Minnie had had tears in her eyes when she saw how poorly Sylvie was. She felt a hot flush of shame spread up her neck, burning her face. Minnie had been frightened, worried. She'd cared! And Sylvie had picked a stupid fight with her. She drew her knees up towards her chin, curled into a tight little ball, tucked away under the sheets. The gang was better off without her. Minnie was right, she was stupid. She was selfish and stupid and didn't deserve to have them on her side.

She gulped in air, breathing around her sobs.

Then she heard something. Someone whispering her name. 'Sylvie? Sylvie, are you OK?'

It was coming from the bed next to hers. Caleb. What did he want? He didn't like her either.

She wiped her face with the sheet and then pulled it back slowly, peeping out at the world.

Caleb was looking right at her.

# Chapter Nineteen

'What?' Sylvie sniffed.

Caleb rolled on to his side. She could tell that it was an effort for him to move. It was weird looking at someone side-on, lying flat. All the shapes on his face were in the wrong place. It was like looking into a distorting mirror at a funfair. He didn't look real somehow. It was hard to know what he was thinking.

'I was wondering what was the matter,' he said.

'Everything's rubbish,' Sylvie said, not lifting her head from the pillow.

'Yes,' Caleb agreed.

He didn't say anything else.

Sylvie looked him in the eye and held his stare. There were purple shadows marking the edges of his eye sockets that made his brown eyes look murky. The whites of his eyes weren't that white either; they were criss-crossed with fine red lines.

She realised that she hadn't a clue why he was here. More shame. She blinked quickly.

'Do you know what's wrong with you?' she asked. There were some diseases that had long, complicated names. It seemed unfair for children to get things they couldn't pronounce, but she knew it happened.

'No one's sure,' Caleb said finally. 'I had a heart operation when I was little. Everyone thought I was OK. Now there's something wrong with my liver. I went yellow. I looked like a daffodil when I came in.'

'Because of your heart?' Sylvie didn't know where the liver was, or, actually, what it did, but she didn't think it was by the heart. Flora would know. She felt another rush of guilt. She owed Flora an apology too.

Caleb gave a tiny shrug. She could see the acute angle of his shoulder. 'I hate it here,' he said softly. 'Now that Barry's gone and my dad's angry it's even worse.'

'The police are here now,' Sylvie said.

'I know, I heard. But they're not looking for Barry, are they? Not really. They're only worried about the painting. It's all anyone's been talking about. They've forgotten Barry.' Caleb's eyes begged her to tell him differently. But

Sylvie couldn't lie. Not about something that mattered so much to him.

'When they find the painting, they'll find Barry.'

'Will they, though? I heard Barry was just used as a distraction. He did that, and now, they don't have any need to keep him. They might have just dumped him by the side of the road. Anything might have happened to him. He's all alone and he thinks we don't care.'

Sylvie wanted to reach out and squeeze Caleb's arm, to try to make him feel better, but the distance between their two beds was too far.

'That's the worst thing about being ill,' Caleb said. 'If I wasn't stuck in this hospital bed, I'd be up looking for him right now.'

She knew how he felt. When she was little, she'd had to be in the hospital much more often than now. Told to stay put and be prodded and poked by doctors or wheeled around by orderlies or just told when and what to eat by the nurses. Taken to the loo while someone waited outside. It had been like being in prison. But she knew that wasn't what Caleb wanted to hear. There had been other times too, when it had almost been fun. The nights when Mum or Dad had slept in the chair beside her bed and they'd told her stories and jokes to stop her being frightened. Or days when one of the staff was especially kind, setting up a game or art activity in the day room. She probably owed the staff an apology too, she realised with a sigh.

'It isn't so bad, you know,' she whispered. 'I've been here lots and some of the staff are really nice. And they all want you to get better and get back to normal.'

'Hmm.' Caleb didn't sound convinced.

'There are people like Davey – he keeps us safe. And Nurse Adams, who's nice, even if she does sometimes seem a bit flaky. Even Dr Malcolm isn't so bad.' She couldn't believe she was saying that, but, well, he had given her the chance to prove herself.

She'd let him down too.

'You just have to hang in there,' Sylvie said firmly.

Caleb sighed and rolled over on to his back. 'You're probably right. But if I was well enough, I'd be up and doing something to help.'

Sylvie pushed back her sheet. 'Well, maybe you can't, but I can. First I'm going to do a blood test, like I'm supposed to. Then, once I've said about two million sorries, I'll make sure that someone is looking for

Barry. Not just the painting.'

Caleb rose up slowly on one elbow. 'Would you do that?' he asked.

'Just watch me,' Sylvie said. It was time to act.

# Chapter Twenty

She had to think things through. She was only here in the hospital for one more night. If she was going to find any clues to Barry's whereabouts she didn't have much time left. She needed a plan. And she needed to make sure the others were willing to help.

Her blood test before dinner was fine. She made a note on her records. Then she went to find Nurse Ratchet to say the first of a long list of sorries. He accepted her apology with a surprised smile. But he didn't really have time to reply because the dinner trolley had arrived with everyone's evening meal and he had to remember who was vegetarian and who was halal and who hated mashed potatoes. He had so much to juggle. Sylvie quietly took his clipboard, moved his lanyard aside and read out the list while he doled out plates. He said a surprised thank you. When they were done, she handed back the list and took her own plate.

Sylvie ate silently. The first part of her plan was achieved.

Next, she had a much harder apology to make.

Food finished, Sylvie crept into the day room. It was empty now. The toys, dropped carelessly on their sides or thrown higgledy-piggledy into a corner, looked forlorn. Sylvie picked up a plastic doll and untangled a toy stethoscope from its neck. She wrapped it in a blanket and put it back in its crib.

Then she took out her phone and called Flora. Her twin answered on the second ring.

'Hi,' Flora said, 'are you all right?'

'Yes. Listen, I'm sorry I shouted at everyone. It wasn't fair.'

'We're used to it.'

'I'm sorry you're used to it.'

'It's all right.'

They didn't speak for a moment. That was the best thing about having a twin – Flora knew what she was feeling just from the way she breathed, her silence, the gaps between her words. Sylvie began to feel the wave of shame retreating. She just wished she didn't need to say sorry so often.

'Are you sure you feel all right?' Flora asked.

'Mum's planning on visiting you in a bit, to say goodnight.'

'Good,' Sylvie said. 'Listen. I've promised Caleb that we'll keep on looking for Barry.'

'What about the police?'

Sylvie rocked the toy crib gently. 'They're looking for the painting, not the dog. There's a boy here turning yellow and he's frightened and lonely. Barry was his best friend. We have to help him.'

'How?'

'I've got a plan,' Sylvie said firmly, 'and you're all part of it.'

# Chapter Twenty-One

Sylvie explained *almost* every part of her plan to Flora. It needed them all to work together.

'I'll need to speak to Minnie, and the boys,' Flora said doubtfully. 'Piotr's dad might say no; he can be strict. And we might get into trouble.'

Sylvie sat down on an orange beanbag in the middle of the day room. The polystyrene balls made a whispering sound as they settled around her body, holding her. 'We might. But I'll take the blame,' she said. 'I promised Caleb, but it's more than that.' She paused, not sure how to explain the way she was feeling. 'I hate the hospital.'

'I know.'

'But it's not the hospital's fault I'm ill. And it's not the doctors' or nurses' fault. They're all trying to make me well enough to never come back. They don't want me here as much as I don't want to be here.'

'I bet that's true,' Flora said with a laugh.

Even Sylvie smiled. She probably was a terrible patient. 'I mean that even if I get into trouble, I'll feel like I'm paying the hospital back, somehow. Does that make sense?'

'I'll talk to the others. We'll do it,' Flora said.

'Tell them I say sorry,' Sylvie said.

'I'll tell them. Minnie will make you say it to her face, though.'

Sylvie sighed. She had a lot to put right.


Mum did come to say goodnight. Flora wasn't with her.

'Your sister is at Minnie's. She's having a sleepover. I hope you don't mind?'

Yes! The second part of her plan had worked. Sylvie tried not to look too pleased. Normally, she'd be furious to be missing out. Mum couldn't know that anything was different about tonight. Sylvie stuck out her bottom lip and thought *miserable, miserable, miserable*, over and over.

'Don't worry, you'll see them all soon. I'll be along in the morning to talk to Dr Malcolm and take you home.'

Mum sat beside Sylvie's bed. Sylvie, already in pyjamas, was snuggled under the sheets. Mum's hand, resting on top of her own, felt warm and safe. Sylvie felt her eyelids get heavier. No! She couldn't sleep, that wasn't part of the plan. She jerked her eyes open.

Mum laughed softly. 'You're exhausted. I'd better let you rest.' She dropped a kiss on Sylvie's forehead. For a second, Sylvie was wrapped in the scent of Mum's perfume, the soft tickle of her hair, the darkness of her shadow. She felt like a chick in a nest. 'I'm so proud of you, Sylvie,' Mum whispered. 'Sleep tight, don't let the bedbugs bite.' She drew the curtain around Sylvie's bed as she left.

Gradually the ward settled into night-time. The lights were switched off. It was never really dark, because the desk lamp on the nurses' station stayed on, and the green running men lit up the exits, but it was dark enough for most people to sleep. Sylvie could hear the sound of regular breathing, small coughs and the odd snore as the children's ward drifted off.

But she forced herself to stay awake. She had to. She slid a slipper under her pillow so that it was too uncomfortable to get any rest. Then, she waited.

She definitely, absolutely, positively wasn't asleep, but everything became a little dreamy. She thought she heard music, then she had the impression that she was dancing with someone who had heavy footsteps. Then they were pinching her neck, but she couldn't make out their face.

'Sylvie.' She felt herself being shaken gently. 'Sylvie, wake up.'

Her eyes sprang open. Flora was leaning right in. Her eyes were shining in the dim light, sparkling with excitement. 'I can't believe you're asleep,' she whispered so softly it was like a ladybird speaking.

'Neither can I. This bed is so uncomfy.' Sylvie pulled the slipper – and a rectangle of white plastic – from under her pillow and rubbed at her sore neck.

'Are you ready?' Flora asked. 'Piotr's just outside.'

Sylvie nodded. She pushed back the sheets silently and tugged off her pyjamas. Flora took off her navy hoodie and black jeans. They swapped clothes.

Then, Flora climbed into the bed. She looked delighted at the adventure. She gave Sylvie two thumbs up.

Sylvie swung Flora's backpack over her shoulder and tugged on her sister's shoes.

As far as the world was concerned, she was Flora Hampshire. She gave two thumbs up back.

Now for the tricky part: getting out of the ward without being spotted.

Sylvie thought *snake*. She dropped to her belly and

143

peered beneath the curtain. The metal legs of beds formed dark cages around the room. Neat pairs of shoes nestled in the shadows. The odd book or teddy had fallen – discarded. The hard floor felt cold against her palms. She slithered forward. The curtain billowed as it got caught on the backpack, but she pushed it off with an elbow.

There was someone standing in front of the nurses' station. She could see polished black boots and the hem of dark trousers, a back in a black sweater. Davey. He was talking to the nurse on the station in a soft voice.

Flora must have followed him in.

Well, she could follow him out. She just had to stay low and silent, in the dark. She passed beneath Caleb's bed, then the one beyond. Waiting for her moment. She got as close as she dared to the entrance. She pushed up on to her feet, but stayed crouched. She was poised. Ready to run when the chance came.

Davey laughed quietly. Leaned in. Said something else. Sylvie waited, hidden in the wings, poised for her cue.

Then it came. Davey lifted a hand in farewell. The nurse stood. Disappeared into the back office. Davey, with his back to Sylvie, paced towards the door. He pressed the release. It clicked open. He stepped through.

Sylvie scuttled from her hiding place. She had to grab the door, stop it shutting. She stretched out. Reached. And managed to grip it. She held it ajar.

She crouched again, keeping her grip on the reinforced wood.

Was the nurses' station still clear?

It was.

What about the corridor outside? Had Davey stopped on the other side of the door? She counted to five slowly, hoping that he had carried on walking and was long gone.

She opened the door.

There was someone standing right outside.

# Chapter Twenty-Two

'Piotr!' Sylvie whispered.

The figure, just outside the children's ward door, held a finger to his lips. Piotr was dressed in black. 'Hush! Davey's just walked past. Come!' He waved her away from the ward and towards a window seat that looked out on to the warehouses. As they edged close to the glass they were hidden from view if anyone did step out of the ward.

'Flora got in OK?' Piotr asked.

'Yes. As far as any hospital staff are concerned, Sylvie Hampshire is tucked up in bed where she's meant to be.' Sylvie glanced out into the darkness. The street lamps were like fairy lights – small, insubstantial. The corrugated sides of the warehouses were charcoal on black. She shivered.

'What now?' Piotr asked. 'Flora wasn't sure.'

Sylvie held up something: a white plastic rectangle with a mugshot of Nurse Ratchet on it. This was the first part of the plan, executed earlier in the evening when she was helping serve the dinners. 'I stole this from his clipboard,' Sylvie said. 'It can get us into any part of the hospital. I didn't tell Flora about this part of the plan because I'm pretty sure that stealing from nurses is on her list of things we shouldn't do. I asked her to swap places with me so I can use it and she doesn't have to. She wouldn't approve.'

'I'm not sure I do either,' Piotr said.

'Well, lucky for you both that I'm here then. I want to examine every inch of the laundry. The police were looking for clues about the painting, not Barry. There might have been something they missed.'

Sylvie's plan was coming together. Minnie's sleepover was just an excuse to get Piotr and Flora out of their homes at night without raising suspicion. Flora was Sylvie's decoy, and Piotr, who could keep a cool head and think quickly, was to search alongside her.

And Andrew and Minnie? She glanced at Piotr. 'Is Andrew able to make enough noise to make Minnie's mum think you're all still in Minnie's room?'

Piotr smiled. 'We stuffed our sleeping bags full of

clothes, in case Mrs Adesina comes in, but Andrew is the best at distracting adults.'

'Good. Let's get moving.' She dropped her head and peeked to make sure the coast was clear.

The corridor was empty.

She and Piotr set off quickly. They paused at junctions and corners, one of them peering ahead while the other held back – just in case they got caught.

But it was as though all the staff were asleep, as well as the patients. They heard distant voices in the stairwell, but they didn't see another soul as they made their way down the staircase and into the basement.

They headed for the main laundry room where they'd met Tania. Sylvie held Nurse Ratchet's pass on a pad beside the door and a small red light turned green. Inside, it had the same soapy, damp smell as earlier, but the whir of the machines had stopped. A tap dripped nearby.

The space was lined with laundry trolleys. Some were crammed full of orange bags, others were empty. John had pushed those trolleys around the hospital. He had persuaded Barry to jump into one of them and whisked him out of the ward. Which one? She rested her finger-tips against the cold metal frames. It was impossible to know.

There were signs that the police had been there – smears of white fingerprint powder on the doors of the machines, an abandoned takeaway coffee cup. Sylvie wasn't sure what she was searching for exactly. But she was certain that if she saw a clue to John's identity, or Barry's whereabouts, she would recognise it.

Piotr kept his back to the wall, inching between the cages, careful not to make a sound. Sylvie took out her phone and shone its torch against the brick. Racks of uniforms were stacked, folded neatly. Piotr pulled out a torch and swept it along the ground. There was a drain hole and some ancient stains, but nothing that could tell them anything about John.

In Piotr's beam, Sylvie felt the same quiet excitement as stepping on to a stage. The space was like a set – dark, full of shadows, waiting for action.

Andrew would be so sorry to miss this.

Did he have to?

With a grin, Sylvie tapped her phone and dialled Minnie. The ring, even through the tiny speaker, felt loud in the blackness.

'What are you doing?' Piotr hissed. He shone the torch up so that it lit his face. He looked like a skull hovering in the gloom.

'The others will be wondering what's going on.'

'We can tell them afterwards, not during.'

Sylvie ignored him. It seemed like the right thing to do, so she was doing it. They hadn't seen anyone down here anyway.

Minnie answered almost with a squeal. 'Sylvie! Is that you? Are you all right?'

Sylvie switched to speakerphone. 'Piotr and I are in the laundry. We haven't found anything yet. I thought you'd like to know.'

'I'd like to know too!' Andrew's voice was a bit muffled, but they could understand him well enough.

'Sylvie!' Piotr looked furious. But perhaps it was just the torchlight making him look that way. 'You'll get us caught!' he snapped.

It wasn't just the torchlight.

'Guys,' Sylvie hissed at her phone. 'Keep quiet. But stay there. We'll let you know if we find anything.'

She gave an apologetic shrug in Piotr's direction. She hoped he understood. She just wanted them to be all together, if they could. She wasn't going to call Flora, though. That definitely would draw unwanted attention.

She carried her phone with her as she continued the

investigation. She kept the others up to date with very quiet whispers.

'There's a table. With an iron on it. Nothing else. A shelf with tea and a kettle. Three mugs. All with the hospital logo on.'

So far there was nothing suspicious or unusual down here.

Piotr's torch danced along the walls, stopping at a battered-looking chair. He rooted behind the cushions. Nothing.

'I'm looking in the machines,' Sylvie told her phone.

'There won't be anything in there,' Andrew said.

She opened the doors to the washing machines one at a time and peered into the drums with their pierced metal cheese-grater insides.

'Was there anything?' Andrew whispered.

'No,' Sylvie had to concede.

'This is nice,' Andrew said. 'It's like being there, but safe under Minnie's roof at the same time.'

'Hush!' Piotr said.

Sylvie looked up at the ceiling. The hospital was above them, filled with sleeping patients. Caleb was up there. And Flora-pretending-to-be-Sylvie. Where was Barry tonight? Was he safe?

Something caught her eye. She turned her phone upwards, so that the light struck the ceiling.

There was a pale plastic vent, yellow with age and stained brown with drips. It was about the size of a cake tin. It was set into the roof above the washing machines. And there was something jammed into a narrow crack between it and the plaster.

'Piotr,' she said, pointing, 'what's that?'

# Chapter Twenty-Three

'What is it? What is it?' Andrew was clearly bouncing up and down in excitement.

Piotr stepped closer and shone his torch up.

'What is it?' Andrew's voice echoed around the cavernous room.

'Andrew,' Piotr hissed, 'hush!' Then, in a whisper, he added, 'It looks like a roll of papers. A bit manky. Kind of brown and mushy. My guess is the vent is leaking and someone has shoved paper into a crack to stop the drips.'

Sylvie looked around for something they could use to reach the ceiling. She grabbed a broom that was resting against a shelf. She held the handle and swept the bristles up into the air. It came nowhere close to the vent.

'Let me try.' Piotr was a little bit taller, but even with his extra reach the broom was raking thin air.

'What's going on?' Andrew asked.

'Hush,' Minnie said. Sylvie could hear the sound of scuffling down the phone. She ignored it. There were more important things to worry about. They needed to add an extra metre to their height.

The machines.

Sylvie gripped the top of the washing machine closest to the vent. She hauled herself upwards, her feet scrabbling for purchase on the glass door, rubber soles squeaking as she slipped once or twice. Throwing her weight forward, she kicked her way to the top.

'Pass me the broom,' she panted.

Piotr did as she directed. Now she was much closer to the vent. She jabbed at it with the broom head. Once. Twice. The papers rustled, but didn't fall. She tried one more time – like a medieval knight with a lance trying to impale an oncoming rider, she stabbed.

With a rain of dust and brown flakes, the papers tumbled free and landed on the ground with a squelch. It reminded her of Eileen fishing the teabags out of cups at the market cafe. Gross.

Piotr edged closer and peered at the soggy mess. 'I think it was a magazine once,' he said.

Sylvie sat on the edge of the machine and lowered herself to the ground. She was still holding the broom, so she gave the papers a prod. Piotr was right. The pages between the covers were just a pulpy mass. No one was ever going to read them again. But the covers were shiny, and that shininess had protected them from the water a little and they were less damaged. Sylvie could tell that once upon a time it had been a glossy magazine, like the ones Mum bought for long train journeys.

Could it be anything to do with John?

It lay like a caught fish on the floor.

'Tania said John read magazines,' Sylvie whispered. 'And she got cross about it too. I bet if there was a leak, she wouldn't have thought twice about blocking the hole with his stuff.'

Piotr crouched down and shone his torch directly on to the pages. The cover shot was of a camera, shoved out in front of a man with a beard. The title was a bit worn and smeared, but it seemed to say 'Photographique', which Sylvie didn't think was a real word.

There was something else on the cover too. The remains of a sticker. It was in the top right-hand corner, above the magazine's title. In tiny print, she could just make out a name: 'John Doe'.

And below that, an address.

'Guys,' she whispered into her phone, 'we've got a clue. We've got an address.'

'What?' Andrew yelled. 'Woo-hoo!'

In the background, they could hear a door open, desperate rustling, then the muffled sound of Minnie apologising. Mrs Adesina was in the room! Would she see that Flora and Piotr's sleeping bags were just stuffed full of clothes?

Sylvie held her breath, despite not being in the room. Were they about to be discovered?

But in the silence, Sylvie realised that she could hear another sound.

Footsteps. In the basement. Heading their way.

# Chapter Twenty-Four

Piotr looked at Sylvie in horror. He flicked off his torch. She ended her call to Minnie with fumbling hands. The sudden darkness was blinding.

But she could hear the footsteps better now. The solid tread of heavy boots. The sort security guards would wear.

If they were caught here then the whole investigation would come crashing down – Piotr would be grounded; she'd be found with Nurse Ratchet's pass and no one would ever trust her again; Flora, Minnie, Andrew – they'd all be in huge trouble. She suddenly realised what a risk they'd all taken in agreeing to her plan. This was her fault.

Outside, the lights blazed on. The guard was close now. If they dashed out into the corridor they would be seen, no question. Sylvie's eyes flashed around the room. They needed to get out of sight, right now.

The trolleys!

There were two in the room. One empty. But the other was stuffed with orange laundry bags. She grabbed Piotr's hand and rushed over to the cage. He resisted for long enough to grab the soggy magazine, but then they were both moving. Trying to be swift and silent, like cats in moonlight.

The cage door was unlocked. She eased it open, willing it not to squeak.

Piotr lifted some bags and Sylvie slid under them. He followed and let the musty-smelling cotton drop back on top. The magazine smelled bad too. But there was nothing else they could do. There was no time to close the cage behind them.

Sylvie couldn't see Piotr now. But she could feel him beside her in the small space. Was every inch of them covered? She couldn't feel any cold air against her skin. She hoped that no toe-tips or curls of hair were sticking out. It was getting harder to breathe. Hotter. More humid. She tried to take shallow breaths.

When the light blazed on, it was filtered orange through the bags. The guard was in the room. Just one, she thought. Heavy-footed. Lumbering. She could hear his laboured breathing. He was a big man. Not that fit. Was he observant?

Don't look, don't look, she willed.

But he was circling the room. She could hear him coming closer. The sound of wood on stone. The broom. He was picking it up. Rats! They'd left it right there, in the middle of the room! He'd know now that someone had been there.

Go away, go away, go away. Sylvie screwed her eyes shut, trying to make herself smaller under the pile of bags.

The crackle of a radio. 'Status report, Arthur,' a voice came over the airwaves.

The click of a plastic hook against a belt. 'No one down here, ma'am. I think it must have been mice.'

'Great. A rodent infestation is all we need,' Ma'am said. 'Do a thorough check, then get back here.'

'Roger that. Ma'am?'

'Yes?'

'Is a broom on the floor suspicious?'

There was a sigh. 'Right now, Arthur, everything is suspicious.'

'Yes, ma'am.'

Sylvie caught Piotr's eyes. They were wide, frightened. He raised his finger to his lips. She nodded silently. She knew he was willing Arthur to leave as hard as she was. Her nails bit into her fists, but she hardly noticed.

She heard the sound of a wooden handle being leaned against the brick wall.

And then, footsteps. And the light snapped out.

She sighed. Piotr's hand circled her wrist in warning.

She froze, but it was OK. Arthur was retreating back the way he had come. They waited in the cage for another painful minute, then Piotr threw back the stifling covers and they both gulped in the fresher air.

'That was close,' Piotr said. 'That broom was a giveaway.'

Sylvie clambered out of the cage, trying to stay silent. It was her fault that they'd nearly been caught. She'd called Minnie. She'd wanted them all to feel involved, part of something. But it was a stupid risk to take. And she'd left the broom in the middle of the floor.

Her shoulders drooped. She stared at her feet. Her shoes were shiny, like eyes in the darkness.

Piotr must have known how she was feeling. He dropped a hand on her shoulder. 'It was good work tonight,' he said. 'We've got a new clue. Even if it is stinky.' He lifted the magazine from the cage. Its swollen pages were stuck together in a solid lump.

It was manky.

Sylvie reached for her phone again. She didn't call anyone, instead she just used the greeny glow of the screen light to illuminate the cover.

The typed label was faded and the edges had rubbed away. But she could still make out the words: John Doe, Unit 3, Meadowfield Edge Estate.

'It's just like the gift shop here,' Sylvie said. 'People in the wards order newspapers and the gift shop labels them every day so they can be delivered. But –' something troubling occurred to Sylvie '– Unit 3 doesn't sound like a house, or flat. Do you think he used a fake address as well as a fake name?'

Had this search been for nothing after all?

'It's a lead,' Piotr said firmly. 'And that means we follow it. But for now, let's get out of here in case Arthur comes back.'

They edged nervously out of the main laundry room – the security office was down in the basement too. Arthur might not be far away. But the coast seemed to be clear. Piotr went first, into the corridor, with Sylvie tiptoeing behind. The green light from the running men signs gave the corridor a murky, pond-like feel. Long shadows stretched between the weak lamps. They had to walk towards the security office before they could turn and take the stairs back up towards the children's ward. Sylvie could feel heavy thumping in her chest, as though there was nothing inside there but her heart.

Past the smaller rooms, past the line of trolleys, closer and closer to the office, then –

Piotr broke into a run. Sylvie followed. Up the stairs. Taking them two at a time, until they broke into the atrium and could breathe again.

# Chapter Twenty-Five

The atrium, in the middle of the night, was quiet. There was still someone sitting at the reception desk, and a guard on the door. But the shop and cafe were closed and only a few people sat, nursing vending-machine coffees and insomnia.

Sylvie noticed a tired-looking woman, wearing the sort of soft tracksuit that might have been pyjamas. She was cradling a baby, bouncing it gently to try to croon it to sleep. Sylvie could hear the wordless lullaby. She yawned.

'I should get back to the ward,' she said. 'Flora will be wondering where we are.'

'You don't want to go and find Unit 3 tonight?' Piotr said doubtfully.

Did she? No. 'Not without the others,' she said. They'd taken so many risks, just because she'd asked them to. It wasn't fair to leave them out of it now. More than that though, Sylvie wanted to do things right for once. She'd barged in without thinking too often, and made things worse. And she had to finish Dr Malcolm's trial properly.

Piotr understood. He gave a short nod. 'I'll wait here. Tell Flora? And well done tonight. You were great.'

Sylvie gave him a shy smile and headed back towards the children's ward.

She held the stolen pass against the entry pad and waited for it to click green. She opened the door a crack and waited. No greeting came. No sign anyone had noticed the movement. She slid inside, low to the ground. She dropped the pass just inside the door – someone would find it and hand it in; it would get back to Nurse Ratchet eventually.

The curtain was still drawn around her bed. She ducked underneath. Was Flora sleeping? No. At the soft sound of Sylvie slinking into the space, Flora's head appeared over the side of the bed. Her hair was tousled, but she was alert.

'Did it go OK?' Flora whispered.

'We've got an address. Get the others here first thing in the morning. The minute I'm discharged, we're going after Barry.'

# Chapter Twenty-Six

Sylvie couldn't sleep after Flora left. She lay in bed, kicking the sheets and turning the pillow, trying to get comfortable. But it was no use. There were too many things whizzing around in her head to relax. She threw herself on to her back with a sigh and stared up at the dark ceiling.

When she closed her eyes, she could see herself running, puffed up and pleased with herself, to Ma'am with the CCTV image that made the theft possible. She could see Barry, ears down, head between his paws, wondering when someone was going to come and rescue him. She could see Mum worried that she wasn't taking care of herself. Worried that she was always going to have to watch over Sylvie's shoulder, making sure she was all right.

Her eyes snapped open like a blind shooting up.

She was never going to sleep.

Perhaps she could try to count sheep. That's what people did, didn't they? But there was no way she could count sheep. Sheep were too smelly and stupid.

She'd think about the painting. That's what she'd do. Dame Julie's painting. Feather-soft blues and greys and violets. She imagined the sound of water bubbling over rocks and splashing into the canvas pond. She heard the splash of fish breaking the surface and smelled the freshness and sweetness of the lily flowers.

Her breathing slowed.

And soon she was asleep.


She woke to the clamour of breakfast on the children's ward. The clang of steel lids lifted off trays. Shouts and clatters as children who had spent ten hours in their dreams got to move about again.

But she didn't mind.

Today was the day when she would prove to everyone that she could be responsible. And, if everything went well, it might even be the day they got Barry back.

Caleb gave her a weak smile as she drew her curtain.

She went to wash and clean her teeth, then changed out of her nightclothes. By the time she got back to her bed Dr Malcolm was standing at its foot.

'How are you feeling?' he asked.

'Good morning, Dr Malcolm,' she said breezily. 'I feel fine, but you can never be too sure. Do you mind if I do a blood test now?'

His mouth twitched, the start of a grin. He squished it before it was fully formed. 'Of course,' he said, 'I'm happy to wait.'

He watched intently but said nothing as she did the test. She didn't pause before pricking her own finger, not even for one tiny second. In just under a minute, she was writing the result in her record book. 'Not bad,' she said confidently. 'I just need to sort out my insulin. And, before you ask, yes, I will rotate the injection site.'

'Excellent. I'm looking forward to the chat with your mother.'

Yes! That had to be good news!

Half an hour later – after breakfast – Mum arrived. But she wasn't alone. Flora and Piotr were with her. And, apparently, Andrew and Minnie were in the cafe downstairs. Mum said they'd all come to see how she was. Mum seemed pleased that they all cared about her. Sylvie knew they did care – but they also wanted to follow their lead the second she was allowed out of the hospital doors! Unit 3, Meadowfield Edge Estate.

'Shall we head up to my office?' Dr Malcolm said to Mum.

Sylvie packed up her overnight bag, while the others headed towards the exit. Before she followed, she stopped by Caleb's bed. He was awake, but looked more grey than yellow today. His eyes focused on hers.

'I'm going now,' she said.

He gave a slight nod. 'Bye,' he whispered.

She stepped right up to the bed and laid her hand over his. His fingers were narrow, and they felt cold. 'As soon as I'm out of here, I'm going to look for Barry. We have a really good lead.'

'You promise?'

'I promise. My friends all do too.'

'You're lucky to have them,' Caleb said.

Sylvie felt her eyes sting a little with sudden tears. 'I know,' she said. 'Hang on in there, OK? Everyone here wants you to get better.'

His hand turned beneath hers and gripped her fingers. 'Thank you,' he said.

She gave a brisk no-nonsense nod. 'Goodbye. Good luck.'

He let go of her hand and she turned towards the exit.

\* \* \*

Flora and Piotr waited outside Dr Malcolm's room while she went in with Mum. Suddenly nervous, she scraped her chair back quickly and dropped on to it. Her hands squirmed in her lap. This was worse than going onstage. What was Dr Malcolm thinking? It was hard to know. His smile was calm and serene. Was she leaving in charge of her own treatment? Or was Mum still going to be fussing and nagging her for the rest of her days?

'Sit still, Sylvie,' Mum said. 'You're making me twitchy.'

'So,' he said, pressing the tips of his gloved fingers together. 'Sylvie has had a very interesting time here.'

Interesting? Did he know about the investigation? Or her hiding in a laundry trolley last night? Her fingers zipped together. She was almost praying.

'Her management this morning was exceptional.'

Yes!

'However, yesterday was not so successful. Reception and cafe staff reported seeing a girl fitting your description experiencing a hypo.'

'Sylvie!' Mum shot upright in her seat.

What? He knew? Dr Malcolm had spies watching her this whole time? And they'd seen her get ill? Her mouth opened, wanting to speak, but no words came.

'They also reported that this girl's friends appeared to know exactly what to do and took excellent care of her. Are the reports accurate?'

Should she lie? Say it must have been some other girl? Or it was her, but she'd just been mucking around?

She looked down at her lap.

No.

This trial was about showing she was responsible. And that meant admitting her mistakes. Even if she really, really didn't want to. She raised her head. 'It was me. And, yes, I had a hypo. And my friends were brilliant.'

'Indeed they were.' Dr Malcolm smiled.

'What?' Mum looked worried and angry, both at the same time. The lines around her eyes and mouth were like heavy underlinings in a workbook, stressing the importance.

'Well,' Dr Malcolm said, 'failing is a very important part of learning. We could hardly have expected Sylvie to get it right first time. What matters is how she coped with failure. And it seems to me that she has great friends to help her out and a determination to do better next time. Wouldn't you agree?'

Mum looked sceptical. 'I would have preferred her to stay healthy.'

'Of course. But learning how to stay healthy requires that she learns from the times when she is unhealthy. And that we learn alongside her.'

Was he saying what she thought he was saying? A tingle of excitement spread through her. 'Can I be in charge then?' she asked.

Dr Malcolm looked at Mum questioningly.

She seemed to struggle for a moment. All kinds of emotions flashed across her face: worry, curiosity, worry, hopefulness, and then back to worry. Then Mum spoke. 'How about this. If Sylvie promises to record all her injections and testing, and we sit down once a week to talk about the record, then I'll do my best to stop checking up all the time.'

'I would say that that is an excellent start,' Dr Malcolm said. 'Let's sign these discharge forms, shall we?'

She was in charge?

Sylvie felt a bubble of delight inflate in her chest. She was in charge! She leaped up out of her chair. 'Thanks, Dr Malcolm,' she said. 'Come on, Mum, we have to get out of here. I've got a promise to keep.'

# Chapter Twenty-Seven

'Where are we going?' Mum asked.

Sylvie was holding her hand and running along the corridor. Flora and Piotr were right behind.

They clattered down the stairwell and out into the atrium. 'We've got to find a lost dog. And a lost painting. And cheer up a sick boy,' Sylvie explained. 'Andrew! Minnie!' she yelled.

Andrew and Minnie leaped up from the cafe table where they had been sitting and trotted across the atrium.

'Mum,' Sylvie said, 'we think we know where the dognapper might live. Do you think you could drop us off there, please?'

'You want me to drive you to the home of a criminal and leave you there?' Mum gasped. 'That is never going to happen.' Then she flashed a small grin. 'I'm going to be staying with you.'

'Hurray!' Andrew punched the air. 'Mrs Hampshire is joining the gang! And she's got wheels.'

'Ms Hampshire,' Mum said happily. 'And, yes, I think it's about time I saw what you lot get up to. Apparently, you're all growing up, so Dr Malcolm says. It won't be long before the twins don't want me hanging around. So, seize the day, as the Romans said.'

Flora linked her arm through Mum's and rested her head on her for a second. 'We'll always want you around,' she said.

'Especially if you're driving.' Andrew nodded.

'Let's go!' Sylvie dived between Mum and Flora, grabbed their hands and urged them to run. This was no time for talking! Barry needed them.

They pelted through the doors. Into sunlight and fresh air. Sylvie breathed deeply. Freedom! And a mystery to solve. She grinned at the seagulls circling the car park.

'The car is this way,' Mum said.

Mum had to rearrange the seats so there were enough for everyone. Once they were all clipped in, Mum's finger was poised above the satnav. 'Where to?' she asked.

'Unit 3, Meadowfield Edge Estate,' Piotr replied.

'The warehouses?' Mum asked. 'Hold on, we'll be there in two ticks.'

'Step on it, Ms Hampshire!' Andrew yelled.

So Mum did.

The car sped from the hospital at 29.5 miles per hour. Mum braked at the turns and spun the wheel hard. Sylvie was thrown back in her seat as Mum accelerated again. Right. Left. Left again. The satnav yelled instructions. Mum's fingers drummed impatiently on the wheel as they waited at a red light. Then, as soon as the light was green, they were off again.

In less than five minutes, she drew up outside a low building. It was ivy green, with corrugated metal walls and roof. The green paint was peeling in patches, making the walls look like a map of lost continents and dark seas.

Sylvie started. She recognised this place. 'This is one of the warehouses you can see from the top floor of the hospital!' she said. Had Barry been hidden within sight of the ward?

To the sound of seat belts unclipping, Mum held up a hand. 'Wait,' she said, 'we don't know who or what we're going to find in there. It might be empty. But it might be dangerous too. I think you should call Jimmy.'

Really?

Where was the fun in that?

Then Sylvie caught a glimpse of Mum's worried face

in the rear-view mirror. It wasn't Mum's job to be so worried about her any more, not if Sylvie was trying to be more responsible, more grown-up.

Fine.

She'd call Jimmy – for Mum's sake – but that didn't mean she had to do it with any grace. 'Minnie can do it,' Sylvie said.

Minnie pulled out her phone and made a quick call. They could hear Jimmy's voice coming from the speaker, but it was too muffled to make out exactly what he was saying. Minnie explained the situation, then made some vague agreeing noises.

'Is he on his way?' Mum asked when Minnie hung up. She nodded.

'We should wait for him to get here,' Mum said firmly.

'Yes, we should ...' Andrew agreed, 'but we're not going to.' He popped open the car door and jumped out.

'Andrew!' Mum said.

Minnie and Piotr climbed out of the car too. Only Flora and Sylvie were left with Mum. Flora picked up her backpack. Sylvie rested her fingers on the door handle. 'Mum,' she said, 'you drove all the way here to find out what's going on. And now you're going to sit in the car waiting for someone else to tell you what to do? If you want to seize the day, then you really have to do it with both hands.'

Mum's eyes widened. She opened her mouth to speak. Then she yanked the car keys out and undid her seat belt. 'Fine,' she said, 'let's go.'

They were parked on the opposite side of the road, across from the warehouse. It was quiet. There were no other cars on the road, and the buildings nearby seemed abandoned. If John did live here, it was a very strange place to choose. They closed the car doors carefully, so as not to make too much noise. Then they tiptoed across the tarmac to the building.

It was surrounded by a low brick wall. Weeds grew up against it and there was the odd empty bottle or tangle of old newspaper. It felt neglected. There was a small parking lot in front of the warehouse itself. Sylvie was excited to see that a dusty white van was pulled up outside. Was that the decoy van Piotr and the others had seen at the hospital?

Their footsteps crunched on loose gravel as they made their way closer. The main door was shut. There were two windows, one on either side. They had been covered from the inside with posters and flyers for bands that Sylvie had never heard of.

As they neared the front step, they heard a sound that stopped them all in their tracks and raised the hackles on the back of Sylvie's neck.

From inside the warehouse came the unmistakable sound of a dog howling.

# Chapter Twenty-Eight

'Barry!' Sylvie said.

The dog howled like the leader of a wolf pack. But there were human voices adding to the noise. Maybe two or three, it was hard to tell. Sylvie pressed her ear up to the door. The metal felt cold against her skin, but she didn't care. She needed to know who was inside and what they were doing with Barry.

Beside her, Andrew and Minnie jostled for a space, both wanting to listen. Minnie, who was a tiny bit stronger, won out. She winked at Sylvie as she leaned in.

A male voice, shouting. Sylvie pressed her ear flat, but she couldn't make out the words.

A second voice, shouting back. Higher pitched. A woman? A child? It was hard to tell.

Especially with the dog. She could imagine him, head

thrown back, ears low against his head, crying out. In pain? In fear?

They had to get inside.

She stood up. 'They're yelling their heads off,' she whispered. 'But if we open the door they might make a run for it. We need to cover the back door, if there is one.'

Piotr nodded. 'Minnie and I will go around the side of the building to check it out. Wait here until we get back.'

The two slipped off together, careful not to kick any stray cans or dropped bottles in case they gave the game away.

Sylvie, Flora and Andrew waited impatiently. Mum stood, still looking worried, a little back from the door. Her frown had the look of someone who might change their mind at any second. As though she might order them all back into the car and let the police handle it. Mum might have seized the day, but now she was holding it, it appeared she didn't much care for it and would quite like to hand it back.

She looked in need of a rousing speech.

So Sylvie would give her one. Very quietly.

'Mum,' Sylvie whispered, 'listen to me. Today is a day you'll remember for ever. The day you save a dog in danger. The day you stand up to be counted. Today is a great day. Don't be afraid of greatness. Remember, some are born great, some achieve greatness and some just grab greatness by the scruff of its neck and show it who's boss. And that's what you're doing today.'

Mum's worried face melted into a weak smile. 'Did you just butcher Shakespeare?' she asked.

'I might have,' Sylvie admitted.

Mum shook her head. 'It was very moving. But I'm not sure that this is a good idea. We have no clue who's inside this building.'

'Barry is,' Flora said.

'A dog is,' Mum, ever the lawyer, corrected. 'We don't know it's Barry.'

From inside the building, the howling became a flurry of barks. Then something smashed. More barks.

They had to get inside. Barry needed them.

Rustling footsteps came from the side of the building. Piotr and Minnie emerged. Piotr had dirt streaks on his face. Minnie had a leaf in her hair.

'There's a back door,' Piotr whispered. 'But it looks all rusted up and it's got plants growing right up to it. It hasn't been opened in ages. The windows are all really small and high up. You'd have to be desperate to try to climb out of them.'

'These people might well be desperate,' Mum said.

Another crash as something heavy shattered against a wall.

'I can't let you go in there,' Mum said. 'Not when there's fighting going on. It's irresponsible.'

'Seize the day?' Andrew said hopefully.

'Not if it's going to get you injured,' Mum replied, her voice as firm as steel.

This was a disaster! Bringing Mum had been a terrible idea.

And Barry was the one who was going to pay.

Sylvie dropped her face into her palms. Why was everything always her fault?

With her eyes pressed against her fingers, she could see only darkness. But she could hear the yelling from inside the warehouse.

And something else.

The sound of a car engine. Getting closer.

She uncovered her face. Yes! It was definitely a car headed their way. Then she saw it. A police cruiser. With Jimmy at the wheel. His partner, Helena, was beside him. The car tyres crunched over the gravel and came to a halt outside the warehouse. Jimmy popped his door open, with Helena close behind.

'What's the situation?' he asked.

Sylvie glanced at Helena. Last time they'd met, she hadn't believed they were worth listening to. But she was listening now. Her eyes were fixed on Piotr, ready to act.

'There are people inside, and a dog. One other exit. We haven't engaged,' Piotr said swiftly.

'Good,' Jimmy said. 'But I imagine you'd like to stick around while Helena and I engage?'

'Yes, please!' Flora said.

Jimmy glanced at Mum. She gave a small shrug. She couldn't object now the police were here.

They were going in.

'Helena, you cover the back door. I'm going in the front.'

Helena edged soundlessly around the building.

Jimmy marched up to the front door. He raised his fist.

The gang fanned out behind him, ready to move. Mum waited right at the back.

Jimmy brought his fist down heavily on the door. The ring echoed around the front yard.

Inside the voices stilled. Only the dog barks rang out furiously.

'Open the door!' Jimmy called. 'Police! Open up.'

There was a long pause. No human movement or

sound penetrated the metal walls. Were they running? Had they made for the other exit? Sylvie could hardly bear the tension.

'Open up!' Jimmy called again.

And then the metal door opened a crack and a face peered out.

A face Sylvie recognised.

# Chapter Twenty-Nine

'Nurse Adams!' Sylvie gasped.

'Vicky, no!' a man's voice called from somewhere inside the building.

Nurse Adams – Vicky – peered out. Her eyes, painted with gold and peacock blue, were wide with fear. They swept across the small crowd assembled on the gravel. The gang, the police officer, the lawyer.

Had she been kidnapped too? Sylvie's mind was racing. Had John taken her from the hospital at the same time as the painting? 'Nurse Adams, are you all right?' Sylvie asked.

Nurse Adams gave a high-pitched laugh; it was more surprise than humour. 'Not really,' she said. 'It's always the way when someone *lets you down*.' She threw the words angrily over her shoulder, at whoever was in the warehouse.

Sylvie tried to peer inside. Was Barry there? But Nurse Adams blocked the door with her body.

'We have reason to believe,' Jimmy said, in his most police-officer voice, 'that someone wanted in our enquiries is in here. Can I come in?'

'Not without a warrant!' the man's voice again.

His shout was joined by a flurry of barking.

'Barry!' Sylvie yelled.

Nurse Adams gripped the door, her fingertips going pale. Then the fear was gone. Instead her face grew set, lips pressed thin, chin determined. 'It's all right, John. This is our chance.'

'No!'

But Nurse Adams stepped back and opened the door.

It was like opening the door to Wonderland. Sylvie felt her jaw drop. Inside, the warehouse didn't look in the tiniest bit boring and industrial. Every inch of the walls was splattered with bright colours, as though a sweet shop had exploded. Fronds of fairy lights curled around the pillars and beams, the skeleton of the building made magical. Huge cushions softened the concrete floor in jewel shades of green and red and purple.

They all walked in silently, as though walking into a candy cathedral.

Until Andrew said, 'Wow! This is bonkers!'

'Thank you,' Nurse Adams said primly.

'What is this place?' Piotr asked.

'And where's Barry?' Sylvie said. 'Barry!'

There was a scamper of claws on concrete, a delighted yelp, and then, there he was! The scrappy little dog, scruffy and scraggly and delighted to see them. He belted across the floor and leaped at Sylvie, a ball of black-and-grey fluff and licks.

'Barry! You're all right!' Sylvie squealed.

'Of course he's all right.' A cross-sounding man stalked across the space. He was tall, with dark hair. And, as Sylvie looked up at him, she saw he had a plaster on his right hand. John.

Barry wasn't ready to stop getting a fuss. He ploughed his head into Sylvie's calves until she bent down to give him a proper cuddle.

'We wouldn't hurt Barry,' Nurse Adams said. 'We're anarchists, not monsters.'

'Anarchists?' Mum repeated.

'What's an anarchist?' Flora asked. She dipped down too and gave Barry a very firm pat on the head. He wiggled with delight.

'Anarchists want to destroy the system,' Mum said.

'Not destroy, challenge!' John said.

Sylvie had no idea what they were talking about. She had a happy, safe dog trying his best to sit on her lap and lick her face. She wrapped her arms tight around him. She'd kept her promise to Caleb. Her heart thumped hard with the joy of it.

'Stop!' Jimmy yelled.

Sylvie's head snapped up.

What was wrong?

It was John. He had turned on his heels and was running towards the back of the warehouse. He leaped tea chests painted with gold leaf. He flew straight past an easel, pushing it out of his way. It clattered to the ground, wood snapping.

Jimmy was after him. Minnie and Piotr too. They raced across the warehouse floor; the crash of their foot-steps echoing up through the rafters sounded like an army on the run.

He was going to get away.

John reached the far door. He slammed his hands down on the push bar and surged forward.

Only to be knocked down, flat on to his back.

Helena had rugby-tackled him. Grabbing him low around the waist, jabbing with her shoulder, she forced him down. They landed with a heavy thud. Jimmy, Piotr and Minnie were there in seconds, adding their weight to the pile.

John was buried under a mass of bodies. He was going nowhere.

'They've got him, Barry!' Sylvie whispered in glee to the dog, who thumped his tail.

'Let him go!' Nurse Adams yelled, strong and clear. 'Let him go, or the Minet gets it!'

Sylvie stood slowly.

Nurse Adams had lifted a canvas from the wall. Sylvie recognised the blues and greens feathered across the lily pond. The stolen painting.

In the other hand, Nurse Adams held a screwdriver, ready to stab.

# Chapter Thirty

'I said let John go!' Nurse Adams cried.

Barry howled at Sylvie's feet.

Sylvie didn't know what to do.

At one end of the room, John had been captured and was facing arrest. But at the other end of the room, the picture all the adults had been looking for was being threatened.

Would Jimmy really let Barry's kidnapper go for a painting?

A multi-million-pound painting, Sylvie reminded herself. Adults had a funny sense of priorities sometimes.

'Don't do anything hasty,' Jimmy shouted.

'It's too late!' Nurse Adams replied. The sharp edge of the screwdriver hovered shakily above the canvas. 'Let John go, or this painting will be rags!'

Jimmy stood slowly. He nudged Piotr and Minnie to do the same.

Sylvie picked up Barry and held him tight. Was Jimmy really letting John go?

Helena stood next.

There was no one holding John now. He lifted his head and checked round. Jimmy and Helena made no move. John pushed himself up slowly. He dusted himself down and gave Helena a crooked smile – before he dashed back across the warehouse towards Nurse Adams.

Sylvie's fingers entwined themselves in Barry's fur. Jimmy really had let John go.

Then she saw Jimmy give Helena the ghost of a wink. Her hand slid down towards her radio. Ever so gently she pushed a button on its side.

John didn't notice. He leaped cushions and paints and skidded to a halt beside Nurse Adams.

'Thanks!' he said. 'Let's get out of here. Pass me the painting.' He reached out for the Minet.

Nurse Adams's grip on the canvas – and the screwdriver – tightened. Her feet padded up and down on the ground as though preparing for action.

'Vicky,' John said in a calm, reassuring voice, 'don't do anything stupid.'

'John,' Nurse Adams replied, 'the whole point of this was to do something stupid. To do something so daring, so provocative, that it would be a work of art! Something that will get people talking about art the way they talk about football results, or last night's telly. The whole reason we took the Minet was to destroy it as a wonderful statement.'

John raised both his hands, as though soothing her through the air. 'Yes, but, darling, think how valuable that painting is. And now it's ours.'

They wanted to destroy it?

Sylvie couldn't believe it. Why would anyone want to ruin a beautiful painting? One that made you feel a little bit better when everything around you was confusing and horrid and grump-making?

And this didn't seem to be a place that belonged to people who hated art. They had made a sludge-green warehouse feel like a magical forest.

'You can't hurt the painting. It's so pretty!' Sylvie said.

Nurse Adams looked at her sorrowfully. 'That's the reason why I have to. People only care about things when they're gone. Do you know how many thousands of people walk past this without even noticing? It's a scandal. But the real scandal will come when it's gone for good.

This town will be aflame. People will rush to galleries to see their treasures because they'll know it might all be gone in an instant.'

A sudden crunch made them both turn.

Jimmy, edging closer, had stood on a broken palette. He froze as Nurse Adams's glance fell on him.

'Stay back!' she said, raising the screwdriver. 'Stay away!'

But Jimmy wasn't the only one headed towards Nurse Adams and the painting – John was right beside her too. 'Vicky,' he said softly, 'think about this. I know that's what we said, but now we've got the painting, we can sell it. It's worth an absolute fortune! We'll be rich. We can go off to an island somewhere and make art and swim and eat lovely food. You and me together.'

Nurse Adams took a step backwards. 'We've been over this,' she snapped. 'I'm not going to argue about it any more. We stick to the original plan.'

So that was what the yelling had been about. John wanted to change their plan.

Well, their whole plan had fallen apart now that the gang was there – and Jimmy and Mum and Helena too! There was no way that Nurse Adams and John could get away.

And that was when John moved.

He dived, not towards an exit, but down to the ground. He rolled across the hard floor. Grabbed at something. Yelled as he pulled. 'Go, Vicky! Run!'

He was holding a sunken handle. A trapdoor. He opened it. A dark square appeared in the middle of the floor. Sylvie could just make out the top set of steps, leading down into the blackness. A cellar!

Nurse Adams moved quickly. Like a ninja or a cat burglar, one minute she was standing in the middle of the warehouse with the painting, the next, she was gone. John slammed the trapdoor closed behind her. He lay on it, panting.

It had all happened in an instant.

Before anyone could react, John reached blindly with one arm and grabbed a can of paint – the nearest weapon to hand. 'Anyone moves and they get burnt sienna'd,' he said.

'Charge!' Andrew yelled.

# Chapter Thirty-One

The rust-coloured paint arced through the air in a gory ribbon. It splatted Andrew right in the chest, splashing on to his glasses, dripping on to his shoes.

'Argh!' Andrew didn't stop, didn't even slow down. Gloops of burnt sienna were flung high into the air as he collided with John. The can flew upwards, showering them both. Within moments, the struggle looked like mud wrestling. Until John lunged for a tin of purple; then it looked like wrestling in melted sweets.

Minnie was the next to dive in. Her hands and arms were lathered purple and red; streaks splashed her face as she tried to pull John off the trapdoor.

John, sprawled firmly over the escape route, managed to grab two more pots of paint. Andrew and Minnie swam in blue and green, wiping it from their mouths.

Their clothes clung wetly to their bodies. All three were living canvases.

'Get off!' Andrew yelled, tugging at John's arm. It was slippery with paint. Andrew staggered backwards.

'Shift!' Minnie insisted, trying to bulldoze John out of the way with both arms.

But he was too big, too heavy and too covered in paint for Minnie to get a good grip. It was like wrestling a giant fish. They all slapped and slid around the floor in a rainbow of colour.

Nurse Adams was getting away.

There was only one thing Sylvie could do. She put Barry down.

And dived straight on to the pile of squirming limbs.

'We need to push together!' she yelled. 'One, two, three, push!' She pressed her palms against John's struggling shoulders. 'One, two, three, push!' she cried again. This time Minnie shoved too. 'One, two, three, push!' Andrew threw his weight behind the effort.

Then new hands joined the fray – Mum! She'd dropped to the floor, right in the middle of the paint puddles and pandemonium, and was doing her very best to dislodge John. She dropped her shoulder, like a rugby player, and caught Sylvie's eye. 'Now!' Mum shouted.

They all heaved –

– and John slid off the trapdoor and whooshed across the concrete floor, leaving a flamboyant streak of colour behind him, a human paintbrush. Jimmy and Helena were there to catch him.

Helena whipped handcuffs on to him before he could wriggle away.

Andrew snatched up the trapdoor. The smell of damp earth wafted up, masking the smell of chalky paint that now covered them all.

He grinned at Sylvie. 'Ladies first,' he said.

So Sylvie stepped down into the gloom.

There was a short flight of concrete steps. At the bottom was a cellar with roughly plastered walls that bulged as though the earth was pressing on them from behind. It was a small space – much smaller than the room above, just a storage space really. A few plastic boxes were stacked, higgledy-piggledy, in one corner. It was impossible to make out what was inside; the light was too dim. There was no sign of Nurse Adams.

The others clattered down the steps behind her. 'Where did she go?' Minnie asked.

They fanned out. Sylvie realised Mum had come down the steps too. She had to duck her head, the ceiling was so low. But she was as keen as they were to find Nurse Adams. Barry scampered down the steps behind her.

'Here!' Piotr called. He was nearer the boxes. Just behind them was another short flight of steps, going up. He raced up and put both palms flat against the ceiling. He pushed. A square of ceiling rose, ever so slightly – another trapdoor! The cellar was an escape route out of the building. And Nurse Adams had a head start on them!

Minnie rushed straight to Piotr's side and together they lifted the door. Rays of sunlight stabbed down into the darkness. A rustle of dirt showered on to the ground. Then the door flew open with a crack.

They all dashed up and out. And found themselves outside the warehouse, standing on the gravel drive.

Nurse Adams was still in sight.

She was near the white van they had seen earlier. Its back doors were open and she was pulling objects out and throwing them on to the ground, like a terrier digging for bones. Barry trotted over to the van, his barks short and sharp like gunshots.

Nurse Adams swung something at the dog – an iron bar? No. A tripod. A camera on the end of a tripod. She was filming him! Then she clicked out the tripod's legs and thumped it on to the ground. 'There needs to be a record of this. This is an important moment!' she cried.

The gang, plus Mum, edged closer to the van. The paint streaks across their clothes and faces made them look like commandos, prowling through undergrowth.

Sylvie could see what was happening now. The painting was leaned up against the van door. There was a camera, its red light twinkling, inside the van, and another outside on the tripod. Nurse Adams wanted to record the destruction of the painting from all angles. She was still holding the screwdriver like a dagger in her right hand.

'Nurse Adams! Vicky!' Sylvie called.

Nurse Adams flashed a look over at them. 'No John?' she asked. 'Good. As soon as he had the painting, he stopped caring about art and started thinking about money. It's better I do this alone. Though you are all excellent witnesses. Especially Ms Hampshire. You're a lawyer, aren't you?'

'Yes.'

'Good. Perfect. You can tell reporters and police and everyone that I'm not a thief, or a vandal – I'm an artist. And this is a sacrifice for art.' She raised the steel point with both hands.

'Wait!' Sylvie said. 'Wait!'

Nurse Adams paused, but didn't lower her hands.

Sylvie tried to calm her mind, to breathe as she would before stepping onstage. She had one chance to reach Nurse Adams, and she had one chance to get it right.

'That painting,' she said softly, 'has saved me when I felt all alone. When I was frightened, or angry, it was like a friend.' Her eyes passed over Andrew, over Minnie and Piotr, and over her sister, Flora. 'Whenever I thought no one cared, I would lash out, I'd be rude or spiky or difficult. It was my way to protect myself. To hurt other people before they could hurt me. But over the last year, I've realised that if you give people a chance, they want to help. You've helped. Dr Malcolm has helped. And that painting has helped too. And not just me. Think how many patients there are at that hospital who have needed somewhere to rest, and being able to sit in front of that painting has given them that. It's a harbour in a storm.'

In the distance, Sylvie heard a siren. Getting closer.

Nurse Adams's fingers laced around the handle, adjusting their grip.

'That painting is beautiful,' Sylvie said, 'and it has given hope to so many people.' She stepped closer to Nurse Adams. 'Don't take that hope away.' Sylvie rested her fingers lightly on Nurse Adams's elbow, lowering her arm. 'Please,' Sylvie said, 'please don't.'

Three police cars, their sirens blaring, pulled up on the kerb, on the drive, in the street.

With a sob, Nurse Adams dropped her weapon.

# Chapter Thirty-Two

'I can't stay long,' Sylvie said.

Caleb raised an eyebrow questioningly.

'I have to go down and be interviewed in front of the Minet. It's surrounded by guards.'

'And there are cameras,' Minnie said pointedly.

'But we'll come back later,' Flora added. 'At visiting time.'

Caleb smiled. There was a black-and-grey dog curled up on his bed. Barry's eyes were closed tight and he was snoring a little. 'We're fine,' Caleb said.

He still looked a bit grey, but there was more rose in his cheeks. When he'd seen Barry scamper on to the ward, he'd flushed bright red with pleasure, and it was taking a long time to fade.

'My dad will be here later too,' Caleb added. 'I'm going to ask if Barry can come home with us, when I get to go home.'

'When will that be?' Sylvie asked.

Caleb's hand reached down and stroked the sleeping dog. 'I don't know,' he said. 'But Barry can stay here with me until I go. Nurse Ratchet said so.'

'Nurse Ratchet?' Sylvie asked doubtfully.

Caleb gave the ghost of a wink. 'The hospital isn't as bad as you think.'

# Chapter Thirty-Three

Piotr was watching Sylvie. She and Flora were curled up, two peas in a pod, in the window seat of Minnie's mum's salon. Their heads were bent over Sylvie's phone, red hair tangling together like something from a storybook.

'The video has had over ten thousand hits!' Sylvie shrieked.

'How many of those hits are you rewatching it?' Flora asked shrewdly.

Piotr chuckled. The stand-off at the warehouse had only happened yesterday. But since they had saved the painting for the hospital and reunited Caleb and Barry, and been interviewed and photographed at the scene by the police, Sylvie had found herself on the internet. The speech she'd given to Nurse Adams about the painting had been leaked and shared over and over. He had a feeling she was never going to shut up about it.

But that was OK. She had said some lovely things. Probably things people should say more often.

Minnie was sitting at the nail bar, rearranging her mum's polishes into a rainbow – red at one end, right through to indigo at the other. There was a place for each one.

Piotr glanced out of the window. Outside, Marsh Road market was busy. Old people with tartan trolleys smiled at children who ducked between bags. Traders called out their wares, took money, passed carefully wrapped purchases.

Then he saw a movement. Someone running. Dark hair, a normally pale face red with effort. Glasses askew. Andrew. He was waving something above his head. Piotr could see that he was yelling something, but he was still too far away to hear what.

'Here comes trouble,' Piotr said with a grin.

Andrew burst into the salon. 'Hey, everyone, we're in the paper. Front page!'

The newspaper in his hand was folded in half. Piotr could see a photo right on the cover: red hair, china-pale skin.

'Sylvie's on the cover, you mean,' Minnie said.

'Nope.' Andrew unfolded the whole thing. Now the

image was complete. The five members of the Marsh Road Investigators were standing side by side, smiling out of the photo. One of the shots that had been taken at the warehouse. The headline above read 'Local kids foil art thieves'. Andrew grinned like a Cheshire cat at an ice-cream parlour. 'We're all famous!' he said with a delighted sigh.

Better than that, Piotr thought, they were all famous *together*. And whatever happened next, to any of them or their families, whether Sylvie became a famous actress, or Flora became a prizewinning scientist, or Andrew ran his own film studio, or Minnie travelled the world – whatever they ended up doing, they would always be friends.

Piotr wanted to say so. But that wasn't his style. Instead, he took the paper from Andrew and walked over to one of the salon chairs. He took a pair of scissors from the little shelf in front of the mirror and carefully cut out the photo of them all. He folded it and tucked it into his pocket. He was never going to throw it away.

'Hey!' Andrew said indignantly. 'You've ruined my paper.'

'I'll buy you a new one. In fact, I'll buy a copy for all of you. And then doughnuts at Eileen's cafe. Who's in?'

And, as it turned out, they all were.

Read on for some
# top-secret character stats
on the Marsh Road
investigators!

# FLORA HAMPSHIRE

Good things come in small packages, and there are few people as good as the youngest twin (by five minutes) Flora. She's always ready with a kind word, or a helping hand, or a disgusting fact if that's what the situation calls for. Her book of forensic science is never far from reach. And her note-taking is the very best in the business.

| | |
|---|---|
| Brain power: | **10** |
| Friendship factor: | **9** |
| Honesty: | **9** |
| Bravery: | **6** |
| Sleuthing: | **9** |
| Self-confidence: | **4** |

## SYLVIE HAMPSHIRE

The older of the two twins (by five minutes), Diva is Sylvie Hampshire's middle name. As a promising young actress, she demands the limelight. She'd rather be making waves than making friends. As long as her blood sugar is fine, there's nothing that can stop her getting to the top. It's been that way ever since Mum and Dad split up.

Brain power: **7**

Friendship factor: **3**

Honesty: **4**

Bravery: **9**

Sleuthing: **6**

Self-confidence: **10**

# PIOTR DOMEK

Somehow, to his surprise, Piotr leads the gang of investigators. He isn't sure quite how that happened – the job just landed on him. Luckily, he wasn't hurt. Now he has to put down his comic books and pick up the reins. Who knows where he might end up?

Brain power: **8**

Friendship factor: **9**

Honesty: **10**

Bravery: **9**

Sleuthing: **8**

Self-confidence: **5**

# MINNIE ADESINA

Minnie is as tall and as prickly as the branches of a holly tree, but her heart is firmly in the right place. Once she's your friend, she's your friend forever. On rainy days, when there's no mystery to be solved, Minnie can be found treating Mum's nail polishes like magic potions. It almost counts as a hobby.

Brain power: **7**

Friendship factor: **10**

Honesty: **6**

Bravery: **9**

Sleuthing: **7**

Self-confidence: **8**

# ANDREW JONES

The whole world is a stage, as far as Andrew is concerned, and he is the leading man. And every other role too, if he can get his hands on the script. He loves to be the centre of attention and is always ready to take a risk. In his less dramatic moments, he helps take care of his mum.

| | |
|---|---|
| Brain power: | **7** |
| Friendship factor: | **8** |
| Honesty: | **5** |
| Bravery: | **10** |
| Sleuthing: | **8** |
| Self-confidence: | **9** |